BEDLAM

THE LIFE & MIND OF EARL SEDGWICK

BOBBY SPEARS JR.

Kingston Imperial

Bedlam: The Life & Mind of Earl Sedgwick Copyright © 2021 by Bobby Spears, Jr.

Rights Department, 144 North 7th Street, #255 Brooklyn N.Y. 11249

Published by Kingston Imperial, LLC

www.kingstonimperial.com

Printed in China

First Edition

Book and Jacket Design: Damion Scott and PiXiLL Designs

Cataloging in Publication data is on file with the library of Congress

Hardcover ISBN: 9781954220089

Ebook ISBN: 9781954220096

AUTHOR'S NOTE

Everything you are about to read in this book is true. It all happened. Every detail. Every twist. Every turn. Exactly how it is written. However, I must admit, it didn't all happen to me. So yes, this is a *true* story, but it is not all *my* true story. I think that's important for me to state up front. Many readers will wonder and assume which anecdotes are drawn from first-person accounts and which are drawn from hearsay or what I simply made up out of thin air. Let me assure you, I have a great imagination; however, the things that I have witnessed in over two decades in the mental health profession allow me the privilege (or is it the responsibility?) to recount some of the strangest tales you can imagine without much embellishment. Whether dragging dead bodies out of buildings at two in the morning or fishing prosthetics out of sewers at two in the afternoon, I have seen and heard just about everything you can imagine. Honestly, the origin of each story is inconsequential as I did not write this to pass judgment on anyone's struggle, pain, or failures. I did not write this to necessarily shock you either. I was literally compelled to write this, and I didn't want any individual to have to answer for their life's choices and missteps. My hope is that this book sheds light on a troubling world. I hope it provides a perspective on the human condition. I wrote this because I was angry and tired and looking for answers as to why these things had happened to me and the people I knew and loved. It's a window into what makes us tick and, ultimately, what makes us fall apart. I am no expert. I am a simple observer, and I believe that most of you have no idea that this world even exists. Even though you pass by it every day. You pass by the homeless, the clients, the staff, and the buildings every day of your lives, on the corner, on the bus, at the convenience store, but you don't see us. We are invisible to you. It's not your fault. Society conditions us not to see each other's pain. We are conditioned not to acknowledge each other's suffering. Even worse, many in my community, the black community, are trained not to admit or display the pain they themselves are suffering from. It isn't OK for us not to be OK.

So my sympathy—no, my empathy—for the mentally disabled drove me to write. I was frustrated by a system that seemed more interested in bureaucracy than people. As I looked around and saw the enormous toll this business was taking on myself, my peers, and the people it was supposed to be helping, my frustration grew. You will read this in the language I use. The anger and pain are visceral and contin-uous. At times during this process, I considered rewriting some passages with less venom, but I decided that allowing the reader to feel what I was feeling at the time was more important than preserving their delicate sensitivities.

Mental health is extremely serious to me. It is not my intention to make light of people's afflictions, even if you find my tone flippant at times. That's my way of coping, and I am aware it does not match society's expectations. Even though mental health is now a much-talked-about subject, in that you can find feel-good, "pat on the back" motivational titles populating aisle after aisle in your local bookseller or online, the industry of mental health has seldom been discussed. The impact of the industry on actual human beings is never discussed. In reality the industry of mental health is not a feel-good story. It is a dark place of forgotten souls. An underfunded, under-appreciated, misunderstood wilderness that fails our most needy because of bureaucracy, apathy, and shame. I hope this work sparks not only personal change for the reader but also societal change for the clients who so desperately rely on federal and state assistance. The language herein can be coarse. The thoughts can race. But once you get attuned to the rhythm of the presentation, you will see that the line between what we call "sanity" and "insanity" is blurry. The phrase "but for the grace of God" should be uttered by all of us daily.

Bedlam is told from the viewpoint of a man drowning in the deep end of this industry. Like many of us, he maintains a veil of sanity, but out of the darkness, he spews a stream-of-consciousness, fictionalized, semi-autobiographical novel. It is designed to be disjointed. It is designed to be jarring. *Bedlam* wants to slap you right in the face and wake you up. It wants to drag you, kicking and screaming, from point A to point Z in a zigzagging, nonlinear rant. Time is of no consequence in *Bedlam*. The only thing that matters is the evidence he presents through anecdotes, stories, dreams, and nightmares. *Bedlam* pulls the blinders off and reveals that mental illness in varying degrees is a shared experience. It's a common thread to be pulled and unraveled. While the ride may be uncomfortable, the critical point to remember is that through the pain, anger, and confusion, he is not just sharing his story; he is sharing our story. All of us need help. All of us have been there.

All of us are living in *Bedlam*.

1

ARGYLE STREET

That's me in the black leather motorcycle jacket, fitted track pants, sunglasses, and snakeskin Pumas sitting against the wall in LAX quietly sobbing. I left all my childhood friends in LA, following a weekend of celebrating their lives while simultaneously hating my own. They somehow all migrated west—one started his own clothing line; another added a new celebrity client to their styling roster. The last one won a Grammy. And here I am. The only emotion stronger than the pride I feel for what they've accomplished is the shame I feel for my staggering lack of the same. Stagnant. Polar opposites. The tears are easy to hide behind the aviators, but now my shoulders are getting in on the action. Not cool, Earl. Not. Fucking. Cool. I hustle my bags into the handicapped stall in the men's restroom and let it all out. Hysterical. My 195-pound—OK, 220-pound

—body heaving like an infant's, tears streaming down my face. Thinking about what could have been.

Before I unraveled.

Breathe, Earl. Breathe. The truth of the matter is that I love my residents, but these people, these wretched people, are permanently destroyed, and there's nothing I can do about it. Nothing. The system doesn't care about that, though. No. It only cares about its fucking rules and paperwork—crossed *t*'s and dotted *i*'s—and I don't care. Not at all. I don't give two fucking fucks anymore. Honestly, I probably never did.

Sometimes I wake up, and I'm surprised that I'm me. That's weird. I feel like this life has been just a smothering nightmare where one day I'm going to wake and be that lawyer or that athlete or that tech millionaire or something fucking important. But no, my eyes continue to open up to this life that just continues on and on and on, and I'm tired of this shit: tired of sitting here day after day trying not to put a fucking gun in my mouth and swallow a couple of bullets. I hate it: my life, that is. More than anything, I hate this business with a fucking passion that burns my soul. The hate swells up in me and covers my eyes. It pours out of my mouth like the vomit induced by a twenty-four-hour viral infection. It's a hate that explodes my head. I sit here day after day trying to figure out what the fuck happened to me: How did I get here, and what on God's green earth am I doing? Why can't I move forward? Why am I just . . . stuck?

Is it the money? Is it the guilt? Oh, Mommy and Daddy would be sad if I sold this goddamned thing, but fuuuuuck, I can't take this mind-numbing, soul-crushing slow death any longer. These crazy people, these ignorant employees, these moronic inspectors, and caseworkers, and doctors,

and

and

and

and . . .

So here I am, crying like a little bitch in an airport bathroom stall. Heaving. Looking around as the shadows disappear from my view underneath the stall door. Finally alone. It's an all-too-familiar sensation. Desperation. Panic. I see my hands unzipping the carry-on bag. I need a fix.

Pro-tip on taking your addiction with you on a trip:

I don't recommend smuggling coke past a domestic TSA checkpoint, but if you ever do, please remember to pack properly. And I'm not talking about folding your underwear and wrapping your toothbrush in plastic. (Although those are great ideas. Don't want to be out of town with shitty underwear and a stank mouth.) I'm talking about careful concealment of your narcotics so as not to arouse suspicion. You know, like how to avoid getting arrested and shit? If you are a "nice white boy" like my buddy Mikal, you can stuff whatever you want in your pockets and walk right through, but if you are black and rocking an Afghan beard as I was, then listen the fuck up. Cocaine, despite what my paranoia tells me, is an amazingly easy drug to smuggle. I prefer buying a brand-new travel grab bag from a company like Sephora. You can unwrap the package carefully, replace the baby powder with some Colombian nose candy, and rewrap. Voila! You're ready to smuggle. To the X-ray machine (and the glorified mall security TSA officer), the bag's contents look like the usual "three ounces or less" fare allowed by law. Just remember, they are looking for terrorists, not addicts. Odorless and easy to smuggle. Perfect.

So when you find yourself crying about your dismal life in a bathroom stall at the airport, you, too, can reach deep inside your carry-on and retrieve that little bottle of magic powder and stare as your hands deftly scoop a small mountain out of the baby powder bottle with your office key as you lean over and inhale deeply, slowly, passionately. I am not just numbed. I am elevated and removed from this world. Cocaine wraps her loving arms around me and gives me a big kiss. I snuggle in her embrace.

Coated in calm.

Sometimes I wake up and stumble around in the dark because my wife won't wake up that early. I make my way to the bathroom. I turn on the water. I stare at myself in the mirror. I strip off my clothes. I step into the shower. I cry. I did the same thing yesterday. And the day before that. And the day before that. For twenty years now. These people and me, see, we have that in common. We do the same thing every single day. Nothing. Absolutely fucking nothing. We are houseplants. We ain't going nowhere. The world has passed us by. No matter how we grow, we don't seem to change. Yeah, houseplants. Just. Here.

Water. Food. Sunlight.

I own and operate a long-term behavioral health facility. There is an underbelly to our society, if you don't already know. Many suffer from chronic aggressive mental health issues that prevent them from effectively caring for themselves. If they are lucky enough to find their way into the mental health system—through a homeless shelter, crisis response center, the judicial system, or by the will of family and friends—instead of rotting away in a dilapidated apartment or living on the streets, these aggressively afflicted individuals come to me. Yes, me. Give me your psychotic, bipolar, schizoaffective masses, and I will house them and feed them and clean them and make sure you sleep tight knowing that, with one phone call, you sentenced them to a life of pharmaceutical tranquility . . . far, far away from you. I guess you could say I own the loony bin.

My business is licensed in Pennsylvania, where the state inspectors are more concerned with process than compassion. My residents live full time in our building, and we have a twenty-four-hour staff that cooks all their meals, cleans all the rooms and common areas, logs and distributes all their medication, washes all their personal items, and coordinates all their activities and appointments. We are basically their family. We are their mothers and their fathers, their chauffeurs, babysitters, housekeepers. Confidants. They are responsible for nothing while we are responsible for everything. My business grew mainly out of the closure of the state mental hospitals in Pennsylvania; the biggest in our state was Byberry.

Byberry Mental Hospital opened in 1907 in Northeast Philadelphia. In the early 1900s, everyone agreed that mental illness was a terrible thing, and we should cure these poor, afflicted souls. Sadly, everyone also agreed that these crazy motherfuckers should be kept as far away from the rest of us as possible. Subsequently, the doctors at Byberry fostered what I would call a "callous" attitude among their staff. They treated the patients like animals. Literally. They performed unauthorized experiments on them, refused them hygienic care, fed them sparingly, and just fucked them up in general. This resulted in deplorably heinous conditions. In the forties, these conditions came to light largely through the undercover work of Charlie Lord. While working as an orderly, ol' Charlie secretly photographed the conditions at Byberry and published them in *Life* magazine. The abuse of any living thing is something I cannot understand, so for me, the willful mistreatment of the most vulnerable of our species is just heart-wrenching. When you look at the pictures of naked men starving and huddled together for heat—scared, confused, and wanting—the tears well up in your eyes. A lump forms in your throat. Gases and bile bubble up in your stomach. In his 1948 book *The Shame of the States*, Albert Deutsch described the horrid conditions he observed at Byberry:

> As I passed through some of Byberry's wards, I was reminded of the pictures of the Nazi concentration camps. I entered a building swarming with naked humans herded like cattle and treated with less concern, pervaded by a fetid odor so heavy, so nauseating, that the stench seemed to have almost a physical existence of its own. [1]

Over time, state inspectors cited more and more violations. It took, like, forty years for them to finally close that shithole in the 1980s. This is interesting for a number of reasons, from my perspective. I mean, I get violations for soiled ceiling tiles (known as "85A").

I guess that's progress.

The greatest problem with the closure was that there was no plan. No exit strategy. Now, I'm not saying that the mentally ill should have been allowed to continue to live in those conditions, but someone should have considered their ability (or rather, striking inability) to care for themselves. What was more humane: the conditions they were living in or releasing them into the world with no support system? Jimmy Carter wasn't a great president and was easily defeated by the charismatic governor from California,

Ronald Reagan, in 1980. And among the many reversals in policy Reagan instituted, none affected the fiber of our society quite as dramatically as rescinding MHSA, or the Mental Health Services Act.

MHSA provided federal funds to house and care for the mentally disabled. As soon as Reagan signed the Omnibus Budget in 1981 rescinding MHSA, mental health care was decentralized, deregulated, and defunded. Perfect. You may not be aware, but the progressive culture of California has had a complicated relationship with mental health for years. The state's left and right wings agree (for very different reasons) that forced institutionalization is bad. They have long believed that someone should only get help if they believe they need help. Of course, most people who believe toasters are transmitting microwave surveillance beams don't usually think they need help, and without federal funds, the poorest among them were left to figure out how to survive on meager revenues. The homeless population exploded. Not just in California (which is bad), but everywhere. At the same time, the country was experiencing a recession, making the single-income household a distant memory. No longer could "Ward" kiss "June" goodbye in the morning as he took his bagged lunch with him to the office. (What the fuck did Ward Cleaver do anyway?) The eighties—much like the forties during WWII—ushered women into the workforce in droves. The new economy rose from the ashes of recession and offered opportunities for upward mobility to those willing to work later, go the extra mile, kiss the extra ass, stab the extra back, lie, cheat, steal, and if you were an immigrant female with limited skills, you could rent a room to a crazy person.

Yes. As a side hustle to make ends meet, many families rented out that extra room in the house in exchange for a portion (or all) of the disability checks of these patients without a home. Historically mentally challenged. Perpetually needy and dependent. The work that housewives (many immigrants and poor themselves) did for their new residents wasn't much different from what they were doing for their own families, so it was relatively easy.

Thus, community behavioral health facilities (a.k.a. the private loony bins) were born.

That old gray building was standing before Byberry was born and remained alive after its closure—since 1930, I believe—and by the time my parents purchased the dilapidated carcass in 1983, it had been converted from two twin houses into a small private elementary school. The doors hung off the hinges, and the hallways were marred by years of neglect. The wood floors buckled from the numerous leaks springing from the bathrooms, and the kitchen was sinking into the basement. My parents were extremely ambitious or maybe just fucking nuts. These two undereducated, overworked minority dreamers had two mortgages and my private school tuition to worry about before they signed an agreement to purchase the building on Argyle Street with no contingencies. No. Contingencies.

The area neighbors' committee immediately started a smear campaign against my parents' fledgling business endeavor. I recall sitting in our small, dark kitchen waiting for my mom to deliver my breakfast. Our kitchen had fruit-covered wallpaper everywhere. I would scribble on it when my parents weren't around. I guess that's where my daughter gets it from. My mom is a loving but demanding woman. She had a plan for her (our) life, and you were either on the team or against her. In theory, a third-grader wouldn't need to read the vile editorials in the local newspaper by paranoid would-be politicians. However, my mom wanted me to be prepared in case I encountered any shit-talking kids or adults at school. She always delivered truth: well, her version of it, at least. I stood there, silently reading the *Mount Airy Herald*'s account of what my parents were planning to do at Argyle Street. According to them, my parents were greedy, soulless ghouls fiendishly ware-housing the crazy in dank rooms and feeding them nothing but water and bread. At least, that's how I remember the article. Tears streamed down my cheeks. My mother comforted me in the only way she knew how: by instructing me to be strong that day. That was always her advice for her "thin-skinned" youngest child. We knew we weren't the people they said we were, and that was all that mattered.

I stared out the window on the bus all the way to school,

hoping nobody would catch me crying. I cry too much. I keep to myself. It's a habit I would cultivate exceedingly well over my lifetime, cured through copious amounts of drugs and/or alcohol. I would transform from shy and painfully awkward to a loud, gregarious connector of people. Is that bipolar? Schizophrenia? Or is it just addiction? This moment set the tone for a lifelong coping mechanism.

I went to school as usual. I always did as I was told. I was the kind of child who, when instructed to remain in a certain spot, would be found in that same spot many hours later if I wasn't instructed otherwise. I was expecting the worst, yet the worst had already occurred; I was infected with my family's business. There were now two types of people in the world: us and them.

Later in life, I would wish to be traded.

As the plane takes off, I think about that little boy for the first time in thirty-two years. I sink into my faux-leather 17.8-inch seat in coach. Fuck those people in first class. Two hundred extra bucks to crash first. Fuck. Them. Remember when the seats had ashtrays? Remember when everything had ashtrays? My mind is wandering. My skin is prickly. Cocaine will do that to you.

"Hey, sky waitress! Give me a gin and tonic. Need to cut my mania a bit. Yes, a double, bitch. We ain't gonna live forever, right? You ever been in the Mile-High Club? Don't stare at me, little kid. You're gonna grow up to regret everything. Your choices in friends, not expressing yourself, ignoring your parents, not focusing. Everything. Trust me. I know."

This flight will be quick. Life is long. Vacation over. Back to the monotony of me. Homeward bound. I order another drink from the stewardess, still hiding my tears. I'm not crying from residual trauma; I'm crying because I can't warn him. I can't reach out and pull him back from the ledge of despair. I want to scream at him and say, "Don't do this! Please. Run while you can! You have so much more to give the world. There's so much more inside of you. I know you have more. I believe in you. Please believe in yourself."

This all started innocently enough. My mother and father met in South Philadelphia. After spending a precious few minutes at Berryman College, my pops joined the United States Army. He spent a few years in Korea as a military police officer, ate some dog meat, and then followed his big brother Lance to the City of Brotherly Love, where he got a position guarding the Liberty Bell. Not really. He actually rose up the ranks and became the assistant supervisor of the Park Police . . . same difference.

Mommy arrived in Philadelphia thanks to the domestic work visa program sponsored by a wealthy Rittenhouse Square–area hotelier. She rented a two-bedroom house, then promptly subleased both bedrooms and slept on the couch. She worked most of the time and only used the place to eat, shit, and sleep.

The story goes that she kept seeing this handsome guy

across the street through the window eating a bowl of cereal for dinner after he got home from work. One day, she just couldn't take the sight anymore and decided to make him a meal. I have a lot of issues with my mom. She can be overbearing, a poor communicator, emotionally distant, materialistic, and stubborn, but goddamn, the woman can cook. She walked that heaping helping of Caribbean cuisine across the street and bam! Love. I'm not sure how far into the relationship she decided to disclose her former marriage and two kids she left in Jamaica, but soon enough, they were a little family, living check to check near the projects in West Philadelphia. Mom would take extra jobs to save a little money here and there. Pops was content to work his way up the government pay scale. Soon Pops started having a yearning for a biological child of his own, and when they found out they were having me, they were determined this baby wouldn't be raised near the projects. They decided not to buy any clothing for themselves for one year and were able to save enough for a down payment on a twin in Mount Airy, a middle-class neighborhood in Philadelphia.

I was born in February 1974, making me an Aquarius. I'm not even going to pretend I know what the fuck that means or that I care. Seems even dumber than religion, if that's possible, but someone reading this who believes in astrology will piece together a theory. Thanks.

My father's only child (but my mother's third) and a boy

to boot? Oooh-wee! I was quickly given the nickname "the Golden Child" by my older siblings, Marcus and Sandra. I am sure the moniker was said with increasing disdain over the years.

My childhood was pretty uneventful as far as I was concerned. We lived in a mixed neighborhood where all the kids got along. My two buddies were Joey (white) and Nelson (black); we were inseparable most days during the summer. My favorite bike was a purple Schwinn with a banana seat. We played tackle football in the snow mounds of the alley, pick-up basketball behind Steven's house, daredeviled down "Rat Road," and Nelson's mom caught his sister Melissa showing us her privates in their garage after a game of jailbreak. I never really got a good glimpse of her stuff, but I got in trouble all the same. I can remember eating lunch in Joey's kitchen because his mom could stay at home. His dad worked at a bank in the suburbs. We all attended preschool together. Every morning we had to sit still through announcements. I hated it. I still can't sit still. My wife hates to see me pacing while I'm on the phone. She hates to sit next to me because I shake my leg. Maybe I have ADD. Maybe I don't . . . Wait, what was I saying? Ahh, yes, I was having a little flashback—a gentle little reminder of where I come from.

The teacher would then release us, and we could pick out a toy to play with. It would take every bit of muscle control for me to sit still. There were two fireman hats, but I *had* to have the shiny new red one. The teacher's voice would drone on in my ears, and just before I would pass out from sheer exertion trying to keep still, finally, I would get to explode toward the toys. The disappointment of not getting the shiny new fireman hat was almost too much to bear.

Yes, I cried.

I vaguely remember Joey moving away right before pre-K was supposed to end. His dad had been promoted at the bank, and they bought a big house in a better school district. I visited them a few years later, but kids' friendships are mostly born out of convenience, not of deep personal connection. We played awkwardly in his new home. I recall being confused that he lived there now. I wondered why. Why would someone move? Leave their home. As far as I was concerned, we had everything in our little nine-hundred-square-foot homes in Mount Airy. We had an alley, and we could go to Rat Road and skateboard down the hill and ride bikes, and he didn't have any of that anymore. His new home was large. It had hardwood floors everywhere. The furniture was lush, and they had two and a half bathrooms. I had only one bathroom. Three bedrooms and one bathroom. Years later, I would flip houses on the side. My pet peeve would be creating an extra bathroom. I have spent thousands in extra renovation costs in order to create a second bathroom. Those families may appreciate them out of convenience, but they have no idea how much money

I am saving them in therapy costs and cocaine. And so I never saw Joey again for thirty years. As for Nelson, my mother killed him off with one phrase: "He's jealous of you." Not sure what he was jealous of, though. We both wanted the shiny fireman hat. We both had holes in our blue jeans. Things seemed pretty even to me. I stopped speaking to him just the same. Thanks, Mom.

My mother dropped out of school early. She refuses to tell anyone how early. My best guess is fifth grade or so. Her Jamaican upbringing included a strong British influence. In 1953, she was one of the children to greet the queen with flowers on her royal visit to the island. I guess she yearned for those British customs and manners because when a number of great schools presented themselves at our pre-K, she fell in love with just one.

Walnut Crest Academy was an all-boys school founded in 1861. The school representatives were sure to stress WCA's strong history of developing boys into men. The alum included titans of industry, politicians, philanthropists, authors, artists, et cetera. But what got my mom was the uniforms. She couldn't wait to see me in that uniform. My dad didn't care. He believed public school was just fine, but when Jackie got an idea in her head, you got on board with that idea, or you got the hell out of her way. The uniform for the elementary boys was a simple jersey, but to her, it meant so much more. It meant order. It meant belonging to something. It meant that that poor little ignorant girl from Port

Antonio, Jamaica, had made it despite everyone's doubts. Despite everyone's jeers and hate and malice. I might have been the first of her trophies, but I certainly wouldn't be the last.

The jersey was dark blue with five light-blue stripes. The stripes stood for courage, honesty, integrity, loyalty, and sportsmanship.

Shit, that's all she needed to know.

I was enrolled despite the fact that they had a mortgage on their personal home and another on the small business they had started on Durham Street. Adding Argyle Street to the mix was simply financial suicide.

Two years prior to this, my mom was caring for the elderly and mopping floors. She would come home so tired and bent over in pain that she would just crumple onto the bed. It was my duty to walk on her back while she watched *The Jeffersons*, and I imagine the story of a hardworking black entrepreneur wasn't a sitcom to her. One of her many jobs was working at the convent. The sisters had an unskilled nursing wing where Mom would care for all of the residents. While she was cooking, cleaning, washing, medicating, listening, and repeating, the nuns were counting money and doing paperwork. She stopped herself one day walking past the office. She watched the sisters counting the money and thought that while she did all the work, they made all the money. Counting money couldn't be nearly as hard as washing ass. Granted, the sisters were probably running a nonprofit and donating profits to a charitable cause, but you still have to love Jackie's thought process. Most people never figure that out, and those who are able to figure it out rarely do shit about it. She enlisted her government-trained husband to help her with the paperwork and went to the bank, the same bank that Joey's dad worked for. She asked for $10,000 in 1980 to start their business. Ten thousand dollars. Joey's dad was the one to deliver the bad news that the bank would not be able to lend such a "large amount of money" to her. Ten fucking thousand fucking dollars. The bank thought maybe she could get started with $1,100.

"Hey, Jackie, go fuck yaself."

My poor dad thought that was the end of the story. Oh well, they tried, and the bank said no. Jackie, however, had no such thoughts. She made a deal with Pop. If she could save the ten grand, they would start a business. My mother took on extra cleaning jobs and was able to save that ten grand in one year. One fucking year, bitches! Back then, you could buy a house for twenty grand. That's like mopping floors and saving two hundred grand in a year today. Seems impossible, right? Well, that's the kind of person she was. Still is to this day. My father is the same. Resilient. Disciplined. Focused. Hard yardsticks to be measured by. They started that business, and they grew that business. They became the largest privately held residential care business in Philadelphia. At one point, they owned and operated four hundred personal care beds with gross annual revenues of over $5 million. Not bad for a couple of yahoos from the backwoods with no college degrees. Funny thing is, I didn't even realize my parents were rich or successful. Even though I went to private school and they drove nice cars, we were a humble family. I thought we were an ordinary family. They enjoyed gardening. They never vacationed, and we shopped at Artie's for discount clothes.

Although I did think life was easy—well, maybe not *easy*—just . . . I don't know. Normal? I thought that this was how everyone lived if they so chose. Maybe I didn't have enough friends. I didn't understand the awe with which people regarded my parents. Especially being a black entrepreneurial family. Honestly, to me, they were two bumbling fools. I referred to them as the Mount Airy Hillbillies, with their penchant for gardening and squeezing a dollar. As an adult, I chalk that opinion up to "can't see the forest for the trees" kind of thinking. Clearly, they weren't fools. However, when you live with someone and are raised by that same someone, you get a different perspective. I especially and regrettably developed a healthy disdain for my mother. The ignorance of youth is astounding.

My brother worked in the kitchen of Argyle Street and moonlighted as a cabbie (where he was held up). My sister went to college. My job was to be good. My mother would always tell people the business wouldn't have gotten off the ground if I hadn't been such a good child. Seemed silly to me until I had my own kids. Now I get it. That willingness to do the right thing would prove to be a double-edged sword. I held a ton of shit in. A ton of shit. I remember sitting at my mother's desk—the same desk I sit at now—and writing in my journal: *I hate personal care, and I will never do this for my job.*

Cursed myself from the jump, kid.

Argyle Street was a strange place to grow up around. Every day, when other children went home, I went to the business. Basically, I grew up in a mental institution. There is no other way to explain it. Our clients were old, crazy, disabled people. That had to affect me, didn't it? Our first clients were named Daniel Murphy and Heather Brown. Daniel never said much, but he did help me do a report on the Great Depression. Thinking back, it's wild that I actually sat and talked to someone who lived through such a historic era. He told me about standing in soup lines with his father, stealing food, and wearing the same clothes for months. I can't remember what grade I got on that report, but I absolutely remember how he smelled. He smelled terribly. He didn't smell dirty. He smelled old, like when you go to a thrift store. He smelled rotten. He looked dead. The corners of his mouth were crusty with saliva. His hair was crowded with dandruff. I remember thinking that it was no wonder his family didn't want him. Cruel, I know. That might be the saddest part of my business. The vast majority of the people are unwanted. Castaways. I like to romanticize it as if I am taking in all these lost souls, but the truth is we are all the same: me and them. I am unwanted as well. I am a castaway. I have separated myself from society in this cocoon. Society wants go-getters and grinders. I am not that. I just want to be happy. I just want you to be happy. Which is stupid because so very few of us are happy. A futile pursuit.

This is not a business; this is my life, and I grow wearier of it each day. I don't recall what happened to Daniel, but Heather died tragically. She liked to get boozed up, and one day on her way back to the home, she fell off a SEPTA bus. She broke her hip. You may not know this, but a broken hip is like a fucking death sentence to an old person. She died alone in the hospital and was buried in a city grave . . . well, cremated. When people die in the city with no funds and nobody claims them, they are cremated. The city doesn't like to spend too much money on them, so the bodies are held until there are about fifteen or so unclaimed corpses, and then the city mass cremates them.

RIP. Amen.

This business has shown me the gray dull of life. It has beaten me down. I try to remain focused on the positives— the fact that I am helping people and I make good money— but at the end of the day, I am just sitting counting the days while we all collect dust.

---

1. Albert Deutsch, *The Shame of the States* (New York: Arno Press, Inc., 1973).

2

DERRICK ROLLINS

Derrick Rollins came to Argyle Street by way of the
Millwood Commons closure. He, along with twelve
others, came that same day. I got a phone call to drive
around the corner to the old colonial building and interview some people because, well, it was a fire sale, and everybody must go! The Salvation Army truck would come, and
instead of collecting clothes, they would collect people.
Millwood Commons was owned by the Manwell family,
who were a litigious bunch. The Manwells fought the
Department of Public Welfare (DPW) tooth and nail over
their violations for years. Though they often won, I wonder
how they made ends meet. When I got the call, I figured
they had finally run out of money. Truthfully, they had
simply run out of patience.

Millwood Commons was a building of last resort. All the

undesirables went there. People who not only were unable to take care of themselves, but whose providers (that's what we call ourselves) wouldn't take care of them either. The final straw came when a resident at the home consistently refused to sleep indoors. The State was aware of the issue, but there was nothing anyone could do. He simply would sleep on the concrete porch out back all night long, even though he had a nice warm bed. Everybody's mental illness is different . . . what's yours? As bad as you may feel for the homeless sleeping on grates and vents during the winter, you would never think that it isn't a lack of beds that relegates them to this fate. No, it's their mental health that needs to be addressed. It's the system that values personal freedom over personal safety. One severely cold evening, this resident apparently went out on the back porch as usual and went to sleep. He then froze to death. To death. Can you imagine the feeling of finding a guy frozen solid out the back of your building in the morning? But first, coffee. Well, the State came in and rammed the regulations right up Manwell's ass . . . and he couldn't take it anymore. He closed the home on the spot. DPW actually had to go to court and force him to stay open while they placed the hundred or so residents in other homes. The local neighborhood association (yes, the same one that had given my family hell years before) actually recommended my home as one of the alternatives.

I recall getting all dressed up in my new suit and custom

shirt my mother had purchased for me from Satolini's. I put some applications in my leather briefcase from my uncle Milton and rode over to Millwood Commons. The sun twinkled past my sun visor, making it difficult to see out the front windshield. The streets were crisp and new that day. The black art bookstore—which would close in a year—was holding a book signing as I passed. The bar—which would see three shooting deaths and close in a couple years—was open for early-morning drunks. I paused at the classic car dealership across from Millwood Commons. It was more of a graveyard, but to me, those old cars were everything. I briefly entertained pulling in but figured I would go next week and buy one . . . when I would be rich.

I had recently taken over Argyle Street after working for my parents at their largest site, the Tabernacle, for four years. My mother and I didn't work well together. I liked meetings and organization and budget; she didn't appreciate my twenty-four-year-old vision of her business. So she bought me out by giving me the now-vacant Argyle Street. I paid for some minor renovations and even did some work myself. I felt like this was the beginning of an empire. I would be bigger than them. I mean, after all, I was "smarter," college educated and all. It could have been an empire had I played my cards right.

There were a lot of seriously disturbed people at Millwood Commons, but I managed to pick thirteen pretty stable characters. Derrick was a double amputee with schizophrenia. Everybody in our business has schizophrenia. Doctors see thousands of patients with long-term incurable mental diseases, so I guess it's easy just to label it all as basically the same. Derrick heard voices. He told me that the voices didn't really say much to him, but he remained in constant silent conversation with them. He would sit in our courtyard for hours, smoking cigarettes and having long discussions with his head always slightly cocked to either side. I guess the voices were taller than he was.

Derrick's sister Yolanda was very involved in his life at first. Well, she never stopped being "involved." It just changed at some point. She changed.

She made sure he had warm clothing and new shoes and came and took him places. That attention would wane over time, and so would her veil of sanity. Years later, she would only come to see him to take his rent rebate. That's the cash the state gives them out of the property taxes that I pay. Yeah, makes no sense to me either. Yolanda told me that Derrick lost his legs to frostbite. He was a raging alcoholic all his life, and one night, he had gotten so fucked up he passed out on their mother's lawn. The old lady slept late, so Derrick lay there until well into the afternoon. With temperatures hovering at freezing, he lost both his legs up to the knee. You would never know it, though, because he got around beautifully. When people found out he was walking on prosthetics, they were always amazed.

Derrick did a few things to freak me out over the years.

They all did. Sometimes he would like to give his stubs a rest, and he would sit rubbing them in the front foyer. The sight would fucking shock me, but of course, you can't tell him that he is grossing you the fuck out, even if his stubs were all nubby and cut off and no-leggy. I would find a kind way to get him to massage his missing leg parts upstairs. He would hop down off the chair and make his way to his room, all while silently chatting with his voices. They were probably calling me all types of names.

One day I was walking upstairs, and there Derrick was in the middle of the hallway, whacking off. Not surprising. I mean, he was human. He had needs. In the middle of the hallway, there was Derrick with no prosthetics, pants around his . . . nubs . . . and dick in hand. Not just any dick either; a huge, veiny, blood-gorged phallus. Obelisk-esque. The kind of dick women talk shit about wanting until they are faced with the reality of physics. Did I say huge? Because I mean fucking huge. It had to be over twelve inches or something. I was thinking, *Holy shit, man! God giveth and God taketh away!* I was frozen. Staring. It was . . . monstrous. And dude was stroking. I mean, he was going for fucking broke. He was beating that thing like it owed him money. Honestly, it was a little scary. I had to stop him before he busted all over my hallway. A huge veiny dick in the memory bank is one thing, but seeing it explode all over the walls and shit is something else altogether. I forget what I said exactly, but Derrick quietly and calmly put his gigantic twelve-inch veiny black penis back in his pants and shuffled off to his room. I sat there in shock for a moment and went back down to the kitchen. When I told the staff, they all cracked up. He did that shit all the time, they informed me. In the shower, in the bedroom, in the hallway, everywhere. He liked to stroke that wood and didn't care who saw.

Reminder to self: don't shake hands with Derrick.

Other than sitting around rubbing his big black cock, Derrick was a pretty cool guy. He never said much, always complied with the home rules, and generally kept a pleasant yet childlike look on his face. He looked like he was always tripping on acid. I guess that's what the meds did to him. He was flat, but pleasantly flat. It was his sister who was the fucking nightmare.

Like I said, after Derrick had been in the home a few years, Yolanda stopped coming around as much and would only show up to get some of Derrick's money. That wasn't unusual. My residents only receive eighty-five dollars for their personal spending every month (still to this day), but some of their families act like that is a huge amount of cash. And they want dibs. It's like a fucking feeding frenzy every third of the month, for both my residents and their families. For eighty-five fucking dollars.

My residents are waiting for me when I arrive. All lined up by the kitchen counter, they have hope in their eyes. Anticipation in their speech. They each greet me today.

Everybody is full of love and warmth. They want their money, their goddamned money. Greed is good. I dole out funds to my people like it's a 1930s rations line.

The "loved ones" come crawling in like roaches shortly thereafter. Long-lost "cousins" and brothers and sisters, fathers and mothers. I guess they feel like their crazy family member is already cared for (by me), so they might as well take the money (bye-bye). Most of them are crazy, too—just better at hiding it. Coping. Passing. Not as good as me, though. Either way, they just come for the money. I'm riding along, running errands to avoid being in my office, when my phone rings. Dr. John—who isn't really a doctor, but "only a physician's assistant," as one idiotic inspector once said—is on the line. Derrick's latest bloodwork shows an elevated PSA level. I don't know what an elevated PSA level means—actually, I don't know what any of the shit I'm responsible for really means—but he babbles along anyway. I hear faintly through the medical jargon, cigarette toking, coffee drinking, and lung hacking that Derrick needs a prostate exam. His sister won't *allow* it, though. I thought, no big deal.

John is a caring professional, but he has a rough way of talking. He smokes a couple of packs of cigarettes a day to accompany his black coffee, and he is from the Northeast, so he curses like a sailor. I figured I would get Yolanda on the phone and kindly explain to her that her brother may have cancer, but we can catch it early, and bam! Another problem solved by Earl Sedgwick Jr. Oh man, I love saving people and solving problems. John drones on and on about some other issues, but I can't remember what. My life is one long phone call of issues and dealing with bullshit and putting out fires. The deep ocean of despair has an ever-rising tide. We finally hang up so I can call Yolanda.

Our conversation starts out pleasant enough. We talk about the weather and how the impending bus driver strike might affect operations. Then it gets fucking ugly. *Cancer?* This crazy motherfucker tells me that John doesn't know what he is talking about and that she is, in fact, a doctor. "Umm . . . sooo . . . when did that happen, Yolanda? I thought you were a nurse trying to open a residential care facility like mine. Uh, congratulations?" She informs me in no uncertain terms that an elevated PSA level means nothing and that she will not allow her brother to have any goddamned prostate exam. I pleaded with her for an hour on that phone. Her words rushed by faster than the trees I passed in my car. Confusion is when there is a lack of understanding. She wasn't confused. I was. Bewildered. This is your brother we are talking about. In my head, I think of my own brother. The one I watched take his last breath. Liver cancer. Marcus sits up in bed. Gaunt. Dying. Gasping for air.

I couldn't save Marcus, but Yolanda still had time.

Where was I even headed? I had a bad habit of driving aimlessly when on the phone. Whenever I drove, really. I begged her. I'm not gonna lie; I had tears in my eyes. Derrick was a sweet guy. I didn't want to see him slowly succumb to cancer if it was something we could avoid. She was so angry. So . . . venomous. It was unbelievable. You would have thought I asked her to shove a knife through his throat. She hung up on me. She claimed to be a Christian and "God this" and "God that," but that was her mental illness. She was crazier than her brother. "Doctor" Yolanda. Problem was she had absolute sway over Derrick. No, she wasn't the power of attorney, but she didn't need to be. If she said, "Jump!" Derrick would say, "How high?" in midair before crashing down to earth on those nubby nubs.

Since she wasn't the power of attorney, I brought Derrick into my office to discuss the matter with him the next day. He made his way down the narrow stairs to my basement lair and sat in my office. As I pulled out his test results and droned on about how he didn't need to be scared—but that it was crucial he get tested early according to all medical professionals' best advice—he simply cocked that head to one side staring up into nowhere and chatted to those voices. Every so often, I would ask him if he was paying attention, and he would assure me that he was. I knew he wasn't. Wasn't even capable. He needed someone to make this decision for him, and unfortunately Yolanda was that someone. She had already called him after she hung up on me. Derrick signed a refusal of treatment letter, stood up, and stuttered his way through a request for the two dollars I gave him every day. Two dollars a day. Yolanda took the rest. Now she wanted his life. He and his voices and his prosthetics and his elevated PSA levels went happily on their way. Derrick's case manager, Isaac, didn't give up so easily.

Some case managers are assholes. They show up every blue moon to get me to sign their visitation verification. Some barely know their clients. Once I had a social worker supervisor call me to figure out where one of my clients currently lived. When I informed him that the man had moved out three months prior to a nursing home, he was floored. His social worker had been forging a signature from our home for the past God-only-knows-how-long, pretending she was visiting him.

Isaac wasn't that kind of case manager. He was a saint. He pursued Yolanda for three years to get that test done. Eventually, he snuck Derrick to the doctor after eighteen months of no treatment. The doctor informed us that Derrick now had full-blown fucking cancer and was beyond treatment. Yolanda was furious. She made anonymous calls to the State, claiming that I caused Derrick's cancer through negligence. (Thought he didn't have cancer, crazy bitch!) She threatened to sue me for that negligence while at the same time threatening to sue me for disobeying her orders to not get him treatment. A real catch, that one was. She took over his plan of care at our facility, claiming we were incompetent, and declared Derrick cancer-free. Congratulations? When she finally moved him out to a home in West Philadelphia, Derrick had lost ninety pounds. It was obvious the cancer ravaged his body. He was skeletal, a shadow of himself mentally, and I was glad to see him go.

Farewell, Derrick.

Before he died, Yolanda called and blamed his impending death on us, saying we hadn't given him one of his psych medications that his doctor ordered. The reality was that he was taking a generic medication over the name-brand one, a common practice in this industry. It's the same damn thing. Surely, "Doctor" Yolanda should have known that.

I think about Derrick when I pass by the empty chair he used to sit in. Sad.

3

MY DREAMS

I am a child running around with my private school friends. We are playing on a large property with a rotting wooden back porch that overlooks a forest of live trees. Davis Niles's hair is so blond that it's white, and it bounces everywhere as we sprint. I can't seem to keep up with them, and I become exhausted.

I collapse.

I'm at the foot of a bed. I stand up and see my parents are sitting at the top of it. Suddenly, my wife and our new supervisor are discussing the business. The supervisor sits down on the bed. She turns to me. Her eyes stare through me. She leans over and plants a patronizing kiss on my forehead as if to thank me. I rise from the bed and walk toward the closet as I turn and face my parents. I start to cry. My mother laughs at me and looks to my father for affirmation.

Rage. I carefully select furniture for an aggressive assault and scream, "It's not funny!

"It's not fucking funny!"

They rise from the bed and corner me in the closet. My father says we must discuss this at the roundtable. I start to scream, "What is the roundtable?" They move in closer to corner me even more. I'm screaming, "Don't touch me!" to my mother. "Don't touch me!

"Don't fucking touch me!"

I collapse into her arms, sobbing.

I awaken with tears slowly dripping down my cheek.

Depression: a mood disorder causing a persistent feeling of sadness and loss of interest.

Depression is heavy. I'm not entirely sure if I suffer from it or not, but I'm not going to a psychiatrist. I'm a fucking black man, for God's sake. We just don't do that. It's very heavy. I physically feel unable to move out of bed some mornings. The dread I feel facing my day weighs me down. Pins me to the bed. It feels like one of those six-hundred-pound assholes from the reality shows is sitting on me. How the fuck do you get to weigh six hundred pounds anyway? Nobody along the way said, "Hey, you're getting a little fat, there, buddy," or "Don't you think five cheeseburgers may be a bit much?" or "OK, I think ya had enough"? When I finally peel myself out of bed, I'm on autopilot for the day. I can feel my body going through the motions of living and doing stuff, yet I don't feel anything anymore. Zombie apocalypse happened years ago.

I sit at a traffic light and wait for the green. My mind wanders off as I stare at the Schuylkill River beside me, meandering off somewhere interesting. I wish I were that river. That lucky stream contained by nothing. What if I just turned sharply? Imagine the freedom I would experience floating through the air toward that blissful end. Car careening, end over end, while I smile peacefully, finally done with this exercise in futility. Ahh. What difference would it make, though? No. I get it. My kids would be sad, and my wife would be sad, but what difference would it make? Maybe my son would be motivated to become a huge basketball star. All these NBA guys seem to have to push through a great personal tragedy that steels their resolve to succeed beyond all obstacles. Aren't I doing him a disservice being this "great" fucking father? On draft day, he would thank his mother for holding the family together despite it all and lament the fact that his father didn't live to see this wonderful day. Then he would take his mom and sister and white girlfriend to dinner at a fancy steak restaurant, where his mom would order salmon well done with extra-thin pasta noodles and broccolini. She would casually make a smart-aleck comment about how her son was probably still in love with his black girlfriend from high school—"Aesha" or "Shania"—and ask why she isn't sitting at this table instead of the white girl. His sister would sit there screw faced because she wanted McDonald's or Chipotle, and meanwhile the white girl would be trying to get pregnant. Can't let them do that to my son.

Keep straight.

The cars fly by, but I don't see them. The streets and the stores and the people are a blur. I don't remember anything. But I don't forget. My days melt into each other. My life has become a series of meaningless events. Maybe I am already dead, and this is hell. That would explain it. The ability of the insane to exist along this plane is a talent that I envy. Like me, they lead lives of crushing monotony. Unlike me, they don't seem to care. They are content with their scheduled meals and med passes and programs and psych evaluations and sitting and staring at TV and going to bed. How do they do it? Maybe they know the secret to life is through not caring. The rat race doesn't have a finish line, so why are we all running? Why care about the toil of life because, when it's all said and done, none of us makes it out of here alive. What's the point in filling out these papers one more time? I should just burn this goddamned office down.

What difference would it make?

I am stuck on this wheel, yet I chose this wheel. Coming out of college, I could have pursued a career in TV and film production. They offered me $17K a year to work overnights at a West Virginia TV station running tape. You may not be aware, but when you are watching that awful movie late at night smoking pot in your underwear and inhaling

Funyuns, some poor schmuck is sitting there at the local TV studio making sure it doesn't skip or stop. Maybe now—with cable being more prevalent and cloud-based IT programs or whatever—this job has disappeared, but back then, it was available. I turned it down to join "the business." The family business. I took the easy road. I was lazy. The lazy man works harder in the end. I never had to struggle. I never had to want. I don't know what hustle means. I am paying for that cushy life now. I should be thankful for all these lunatics. They pay my bills, after all. Send me on vacation. Buy my drugs. But I only feel envy. Envy that they don't seem to care that Monday is Tuesday is Wednesday is Thursday is Friday is Saturday is Sunday . . .

Yeah, this has got to be depression.

4

NANCY PISTONIA

The stench in the building hits my nose. I hold my mouth to avoid vomiting all over the front entrance. My original administrator's license from 1992 hanging on the wall slowly comes into focus as the staff points me to a room upstairs. I'm used to awful smells like Rudolph's breath and Edward's urine-soaked pants, but this is fucking ridiculous. It's Nancy's foot—or rather, her rotting flesh on her big toe that the maggots are wriggling out of. Nancy is possibly my favorite resident, but right now she makes me want to vomit. Don't know how Tim the nurse is down there on one knee, so close to that shit. Smiling. Babbling away. I have to run out of the room. I want to run out of the building. I need to run out of this life. Instead, I have to run downstairs and write a report.

Many years ago, Bowen and Bowen Personal Care was

closing down. I had been working for my parents at Bethesda Court, but like I said, my mom and I weren't getting along at the office. I was young and full of ideas, and she was being completely unreasonable. Biased, I know, but she should write her own fucking book. When I inherited Argyle Street, I was in heaven. Every day I got up and sprinted to the concrete carcass to restore it to its former glory. Soon after renovating the place, I got the call to pick up a client at Bowen and Bowen. I hopped in our van and drove over. The building wasn't just closing; it was scheduled to be demolished. Immediately. Like right then and there. Earl Cat bulldozers on the goddamned lawn. After finding my way through the labyrinth of a building with no assistance from any staff (why would there be staff when the building was being demolished?), I found Nancy Pistonia sitting in the dining room with a huge shit-eating grin on her face. She was an obese black woman with three layers of clothes on. She had on size twenty sneakers that flopped around her size ten feet. Her multiple knit hats were pulled down over one eye. She was missing the majority of her teeth. The few that were left were black from smoking cigarettes and not brushing. Despite all that, her brown eyes sparkled with a delight that is rare in this world. She had the prettiest eyes and the sweetest smile. She smiled like she knew something we didn't know. Shit, maybe she did.

I sat down and introduced myself to someone who would prove to be one of the most interesting people I had ever met. I told her the building was being closed and demolished and that I was the only one available to take her to my personal care home. She laughed at me. She laughed and told me God almighty would save the building. The equipment in the yard was hers, and she wasn't going to demolish anything. We went back and forth for an hour. I talked about the beautiful building she would live in and all the food I would feed her, plus the hot showers and the friendly staff who would shop for her "food, clothing, and supplies *t-o-o*." Nancy liked to spell out *too* for some reason. Finally, she informed me she "wasn't flaunting and wasn't marrying filth," but she would go with me. It's weird now to think about how elated I was to get her to come with me. I suppose it was this feeling that I had accomplished something her case manager couldn't; her doctors couldn't. Hell, even the threat of death by demolition couldn't. Maybe I had a gift because Nancy moved in that day and never left the property for damn near twenty years—unless it was in an ambulance for an ER visit. She didn't go to the store. She didn't go to the corner. She didn't go to the fucking front step.

When she arrives, Nancy is hilarious. She hates her two roommates. She calls Sherry "Slop" because Sherry is 350 pounds, and she calls Edith "Mo' Murda" because she is as mean as a rattlesnake. They share a room with three beds, three chairs, a mirror, and two dressers. Nancy claims that these two stab her with knives during the night and steal her "food, clothing and supplies," forcing her to carry bags of shit everywhere she goes. Nancy carries two nonworking cell phones and calls God to order food, clothing, and supplies. Oh, and money *t-o-o*. Nancy orders money to my office on a near-daily basis. She simply calls God on her cell phone and ever so politely asks the Holy Father to deliver $200K or so to my drawer. She hangs up and beams at me with those black teeth and sparkling eyes. I can't help but indulge her when she asks if I will give her a portion of my new riches. If only it were that easy, Nancy.

Her psychosis is dangerous. That inclination to claim that people are raping her. People are stabbing her. People are robbing her. When they walk past her. In the middle of the night. When they first walk through the door. Not dangerous for Nancy. Dangerous for me.

Nancy doesn't hold on to money for too long. None of them do. When I give her the monthly allowance of eighty-five dollars, she is normally broke by the next day at the latest. This triggers a month-long series of accusations of who has stolen her cash from her pockets or her bags or her nightstand and then the stabbings. And, of course, the rapes. If the State ever heard her accusations, they would force me to investigate the entire situation. I would have to put staff on suspension pending the outcome. I would need to discharge residents. It would be a mess. That is because the state inspectors are fucking idiots. They are cyborgs sent here from Harrisburg to dot my *i*'s and cross my *t*'s. Instead,

I manage Nancy's accusations, and since I know her so well, I can mostly tell when she is crying wolf. (The lack of stab wounds is usually my first clue.) I say mostly because there is something attacking her besides her psychosis, and it's called diabetes. Sweet-crazy Nancy is in denial of her main medical condition, and it's slowly eating away at her. It doesn't help matters that she will sit and consume cookies, cakes, pies, two-liter sodas, and candy nonstop.

When she began to complain that Slop and Mo' Murda were sticking needles in her foot at night, we didn't pay attention at first. I mean, seriously, we have heard her accuse people of all kinds of shit (I mentioned the walk-by stabbings and rapes, right?) Luckily, we had Tim the nurse check her out just to be on the safe side. Wearing her huge size twenty shoes (she demands we buy them that big) was causing her toe to rub abnormally, and the rubbing led to a sore on her toe. Diabetics—well, non-compliant diabetics especially—have a hard time healing. So when there was an odor emanating from her foot that smelled like death had walked into the front foyer and found a chair in the TV room, we were lucky we caught it in time to save the foot. But she lost her big toe on her right foot. The smell was bad, like I said, but the maggots were the icing on the cake. Seeing that was one of those moments that makes you evaluate whether the world wasn't some crazy reality show or an episode from the *Twilight Zone* where you were the star but didn't know it. Maggots in her foot? Yeah, right. No, sorry, that's exactly what it was. Tim talked to me and informed me that, actually, maggots were a good thing. Maggots eat rotting flesh, so they were actually cleaning out the wound for her. Yeah, Tim, tell that to the cyborgs: "That does not compute." Nancy was forced to spend a week in Willow Crest, rehabbing her foot and learning to walk again. She loved her stay at Willow Crest. The staff there pushed her around in a wheelchair and let her smoke cigarettes and fed her all her meals in bed until she was "better." *Better* in our world means when Medicare stops paying for your medical care. Nancy returned to us just as crazy as normal . . . minus one toe. Her habitual noncompliance—gorging herself on gas station delicacies infused with processed sugar—methodically led to the eventual amputation of her entire foot after the toe. Slop and Mo' Murda had really done it this time. Her whole fucking foot. Nancy wasn't fazed, though. She rallied against them and continued her eating habits, all the while claiming that her foot would grow back.

During her illness, we learned she was a former beauty queen married to an Italian man and had three children and grandchildren. Umm, what?

One day I'm asking staff about Nancy's stay in rehab, and Miller tells me everything is fine and that he gave her daughter the room info. Pause. Daughter? What fucking daughter? I've known her for a decade, and never once did she mention a daughter. She actually prides herself on saying she isn't married to filth, and she is prejudiced. I guess against black people? Did I tell you Nancy's black?

Nancy did, indeed, have a family. Her daughters and grandchildren were beautiful. I suppose her psychosis had robbed her of her will to be a mom, a wife, and a model. Nancy's eyes were big and brown, but in her current state of decay, I would never have guessed how beautiful she must have been. Well, it turns out she was once married to a well-to-do Italian man. His family didn't approve, and as she got weirder and weirder, he simply left. And he didn't just leave; he had her committed and dissolved their marriage, leaving her penniless. They were just another black family torn apart by an absentee dad. Just like they show on TV, right? She stopped caring for the kids and just disappeared one day. They had searched years for her and finally found her here, thanks to a private detective.

When they arrived, the scene wasn't pretty. Nancy would not talk to them. Not a word. Until she did. Then, she really did. She told them she was prejudiced and called the grand-daughter a little bitch. The family was obviously a little disturbed. Over the next few months, I had long talks with her daughter. It's hard for family members to understand psychosis. You want to view Mom as normal and maybe just a little quirky. You can't understand just how far they are gone from our reality, just how much the medication is holding together this mess that you see. I suggested they pretend not to be her family. They balked at the idea for months. After being called "bitches" and "bastards" and "filth" and being spat upon, they finally relented and approached as friends. Seeing Nancy out in the courtyard under the sun, among the green hedges and plants in the garden, talking with her "friends" was beautiful. She giggled and talked and smoked. It was just beautiful. They brought her gifts, and she let them stay.

One day I walk into the building, and Nancy is hailing me from the hallway. She is yelling about how John (a disabled alcoholic vet who may be the only sane resident we have) "libeled" on her that she didn't want to see her family and that he is filth and a murderous thief and all kinds of awful things. I patronize her to get into my office and start attending to the mountain of paperwork that has grown on my desk over the last week. Every time I open the goddamned mailbox, it's more crap. IRS, State Department, city, oh my! My friends call it "rich people problems," but if I'm rich, then I need someone to tell my bank account because it is ignorant of that shit.

After a few hours, I can still hear Nancy yelling. I decide to go investigate and talk to Miller, my best employee who is like the crazy person whisperer. Turns out Nancy called her daughter (her word) and was angry because she thought her daughter had come by while she was in the bathroom, and John had told her daughter to leave because Nancy wasn't home. I'm not sure if my mouth hit the ground, but now I understand the expression. Daughter. Wow. Miller just laughed and laughed. Miller said, "Yeah, bruh. She called her *daughter*. Said she wants her daughter to bring her some soda. Tried to tell Nancy she's still coming, but she's mad at John."

Damn. Nancy wants to see her daughter. That's. Fucking. Beautiful.

Now Nancy sits in her corner smiling—ordering money to my desk, waiting for her daughter and grandkids, and ignoring her doctor's advice. Ahh, perfect. Seems like a great time to take the clients on a field trip. Nancy's happy, the building is calm, and nobody has maggots crawling out of their bodies. My clients love field trips . . . well, they like *certain* field trips. Not the ones to the zoo or to the museum or on trolley tours around Olde City in Philadelphia, learning about the Liberty Bell. No. They only like the field trips to the buffet. Any buffet. Yes, "that" buffet. You know, "all you can eat." Maybe that's why I hate buffets. The knowledge that, on any given day, a horde of mentally disabled, hygiene-challenged residents of an institution may descend upon an establishment is bad enough in and of itself, but to think of the feeble attempt at protection the sneeze guards provide makes me shudder. I have seen my clients in action. Order a la carte . . . trust me.

The vans pull up, and the clients roll out. They jockey for position in line to board the vans with visions of lamp-heated steak in their eyes. The staff is giddy right along with them. Simple things for the simple, I suppose. Everyone except for Nancy is supremely excited for the adventure. Nancy isn't excited. Nancy isn't simple. Nancy isn't going "any goddamned where." Somebody has to stay behind, and I gladly take on that responsibility. I want nothing to do with that buffet. Not only wouldn't I eat there; even the sight of them scarfing the food down and the crumbs and gravy and mashed potatoes and heat lamps are all just too much for me. I would rather keep Nancy company right here at "home."

When they leave, it's just Nancy and me in the building. The building seems much larger when it's almost empty. It breathes and lives and echoes. It is cavernous without the normal cacophony. Nancy sits and smiles as she talks on her phone to Jesus. I ordered her food as a treat since her "suite-mates" are all off picking gravy clumps off their faces. I sit and watch her waiting for the pizza to arrive. I can't say this is the first time it happened, but it certainly was the first time I can recall the severity at this level. The first time it grabbed me and shook my reality.

The voices.

I'm sitting there watching Nancy, and I notice I am having a whole fucking conversation with someone about her. Nobody's fucking here, though. Whoa! A full-on back and forth about Nancy and lunch and her foot and the buffet and holy shit! Maybe Nancy's laughing at me? Can she see the people I am talking to? Oh my God, I am losing my mind. Fuck. Now the stress of the realization seizes me like a boa constrictor. Tightening. It's getting harder to breathe. The room is spinning. Walls perform their best Dali impressions. The voices are getting louder. I can see my brother sitting up in bed. But he is dead. Holy shit, I'm losing my grip. Losing my shit. What the fuck is going on here? My mouth starts to water. This is crazy. Am I having a heart attack? Am I crazy? Probably both. Fuck fuck fuck. The voices are so loud. So. Fucking. Loud. I can't understand them because I'm blacking out. Black. Out. My chest really hurts. I need help. I need help. Please help me . . . Nancy? Oh man, nobody is home but Nancy. No-foot, paranoid schizophrenic, Jesus-calling Nancy.

Damn, I hope her cell phone works . . .

That's me dropping down on one knee. Clutching at my chest. Grimacing. Dying. Nancy puts her phone away. Her face contorts in austere reflection. She cranes her neck and leans over. Eyes narrow. Piercing me. "What are they saying?" she asks. What are they saying? Can she hear them? What the fuck? Is this even happening? This can't be happening. "Just listen to them. What are they saying?" she asks again. She beckons me to stand. Her eyes say relax. She even smiles and laughs. Oh, she laughs. Deep abdominal guttural laughs. She isn't laughing at me. She is laughing for me. Right? My body is trembling. Which side of this fence will I land on? What are they saying? Shit. What *are* they saying? I never listen. Never listened. OK. Calm down. Breathe. I try to focus on their words. They are coming fast.

It's just gibberish. Nonsense. I can't understand any of it. Nancy is starting to disappear. The room is starting to disappear. "What are they saying?" I don't fucking know, Nancy. Maybe . . . oh shit, I can hear them. Hear *him*.

One voice stands out. They are singing to me. Angelic voices singing about love and goodness and my life as it should be. Scary. My dreams, hopes, and desires harmonized. Projected. The world explained. Singing to me. It's beautiful. Crazy and beautiful. What the fuck? Is this what insanity sounds like? I don't wanna listen because I don't wanna be insane. I'm not insane. Voices need bodies. Voices need a source. This is not the way shit's supposed to go down. Nancy's laughing, voices singing, room disappearing. *No no no no no!* I'm screaming and crying, and Nancy is telling me it's going to be OK. She is shushing me and patting my back and laughing. And it's working. My breathing is slowing down. The room is coming back into focus, and the voices fade. I stand as best I can, looking down at Nancy. Trying to look down on Nancy. I can't do that anymore. Is this what her life is like? Is that what she hears? What *we* hear? A tsunami of song that cripples? Pushing her into herself? Suffocating everything out of your body? Your desire for all worldly functions? I'm asking Nancy this. Her eyes sparkle, and she smiles. She picks up the phone and calls God. As I stumble away from her, she says, "Enjoy the ride."

5

PAIN

I'm standing in my pajamas in the dark, listening to my wife's sleeping noises: a melodic mixture of both snoring and grunting. Not unpleasant, yet she wouldn't want a stranger to hear it. I can't sleep. I'm staring at the stairwell. It leads to nowhere; it just goes down. My jaw is in pain. The pain is searing through my neck and my head. The Advil PM ain't doing shit. I'm still in pain. Jaw pain. Is it a heart attack? WebMD seems to think so. Aneurysm? Still in pain. What's new? Maybe all the pain in my brain has finally poured out over my body. Mind over matter. But now the matter is killing me. 'Bout time. I doze off at my dining room table. How did I even get here? My nightmare this evening is that it's pay week (which it is), and I'm broke (which I am). There are thirteen dollars in my account, and I am sitting at the dining room table crying and wishing I had thought of something else to do for a living. Anything else. My brother Marcus walks past the door in his hospital gown. Skeletal. He never speaks.

I wake up in that seated position and call my dentist. He's a cardiologist, right? I realize in the midst of getting dressed that I was just dreaming about the thirteen dollars. Nevertheless, I'll ignore my bank statements until I'm damn well ready.

Getting down the stairs is a chore these days. My kids and wife whirl around the house preparing for their day, unaware that their family may be one loser short by noon. Heart attack. Aneurysm. Bye, Dad. The cartilage in my knee has deteriorated into arthritis, and I cautiously approach and attempt the stairs like a ninety-year-old man. I've aged twenty years this morning alone. I hobble to my car. Didn't even kiss them goodbye. Hope they leave that out of the eulogy. I call my general physician and tell him I'm dying. He makes an emergency appointment. He knows he'll be overpaid for my death. Blue Cross Blue Shield.

My car is winding down Lincoln Drive toward my grave, but first it's gonna stop at the dentist's office to check my heart, then to my GP to send me to the morgue. A minivan is tailgating me despite the available lane next to us. I am in no mood this morning, so I pull to the left just ahead of the huge dips in the road that cause cars to bounce like carnival rides. I look to my right in time to see the driver separate from the seat and nearly hit his head on the roof. I find no joy in it this time however, because at least he'll still be here tomorrow. I know every pothole in this street, every turn of this neighborhood. My car pulls into my parents' driveway. They are on vacation in Florida, and I must refill Mother's bucket for the last time. She has this huge wooden trough at the front door, which she calls a fountain but which looks more like a large wooden bucket or feeder from a dairy farm. Their home sits on an acre in Mount Airy, which is quite rare. It looks like an old plantation house. The story goes that a union general built it as a surprise for his wife, but upon seeing it, she demanded a smaller home. So he built an exact replica across the street. Selfish bitch.

I wasn't too keen on the house when we first got there either. The home belonged to the Goldenberg family, whose only son attended the same school as me. They were going through a divorce. A nasty, knockdown, drag-out, you-fucked-the-babysitter divorce. My mother and father had jogged past the house for years dreaming of the inside, and when it went on the market, they asked to see it. At the time, the house had fallen into serious disrepair (similar to the Goldenbergs' lives). I can relate. I recall distinctly how quiet the Goldenbergs remained while we toured their once-magnificent home. Quiet and separated. The kitchen was decorated with walls of peeling paint, a vintage white Roper three-compartment stove, complete with pancake griddle, grease runoffs, and mouse droppings. The bathrooms featured yellow, blue, and mauve tile with wooden toilet seats. I stole a Matchbox car from the kitchen. That Matchbox car was on my mind as I climbed out of my truck to fill the bucket. Why had I taken it? I will never be able to answer that. It wasn't like I needed it. I had my own. If I buy a new Matchbox car now, can I return it when I get to hell?

I hop in my car after locking my parents' door behind me. I let out a long, heavy sigh and stare down at that intake bracelet from the Germantown Hospital emergency room. Yesterday's incident in front of Nancy seems like it happened ages ago. The sweating and the suffocating and the walls and the voices and Nancy sitting there and staring at me. It was all too much. I had to run out of there and head to the ER. I thought I was dying. Again. They thought it was the drugs in my bloodstream. Again. Maybe we both were right. Thankfully, nobody believed Nancy when she told them what she had seen. Poor Nancy. Maybe Nancy wasn't as crazy as I thought.

Maybe she *could* talk to God.

Now I'm not paying attention to the road. I'm thinking about Nancy and the voices and my life. My pitiful life. And my impending death. Hope the car doesn't crash on the way to my death. Cruise control. The streets of Philadelphia are filled with corpses, hustling and bustling about. I am not sure where they are going, but they all seem absolutely determined to get there. Everybody is so fucking busy. Don't they know they have tomorrow? Police officers stare into my car. Pedestrians stare straight ahead. A ballet of defeat.

The pain in my mouth is intense now. It is difficult for me to even form sentences to talk to myself. The intercom at ZoMe Medical answers my buzz. "How can I help you?" I cannot answer. He lifts the gate anyway, telling me to park in a parking spot.

I am jealous of Dr. George's professional office. Stark walls and beautiful staff, all smiling with perfect white teeth and black uniforms. I yearn to trade places with him. I wish I made better decisions, saved money, took vacations, mentored children, stayed sober, didn't die of a heart attack. Like normal people do. Maybe I would've gone to law school or opened a bar, become a consultant or written a book. Maybe accomplishing something on my own would've changed everything. Something that nobody gave me or started for me or paid for would've stopped the pain. Too late now. This ache I feel. Oprah said follow your passion, but I can't remember what mine is. Is it acting? I was excited to see myself on that TV show, even for those brief nine seconds and that one poorly delivered line. Despite the fact that my wife didn't watch it, and my kids were underwhelmed. I've been acting every day of my life and never got paid, so that $370 meant something. Everything. Where's the rest, though? I do a damn good job acting like a husband and a father. And an owner of a loony bin who cares about his residents. Where's my fucking Oscar?

I open my eyes. Dr. George looks like a vampire. His eyes are piercing. Teeth are perfect. His hair is jet black with strategic streaks of gray. As he enters the examination room, his coat flows behind him. He takes a look at me. "Your face is twice its size," he says. How would I know? I haven't looked in a mirror in months. With seemingly one motion, he grabs his tools and stool and starts working on my mouth. He hits a nerve. I might blackout. Abscess. At least I knew it began with an *A*. I survived. There's still hope from Dr. Lawrence, though.

Dr. Lawrence's office is smaller than Dr. George's. Like a coffin. Comfy. I'm sweating and scared. I should be celebrating. Should've picked up my penicillin prescription before coming here. Could've OD'd in the waiting room. My heart is beating fast. I'm impressed it's still working.

Dr. Lawrence listens to me tell my story—well, part of my story. I leave out the drugs and the mommy issues and the job despisement and the voices. He also doesn't know I came here to die. I just survived an aneurysm, though. Heart attack to come. His nurse places suction cups all over my upper torso. Wired dots haphazardly scattered about. I look ridiculous. They leave me alone to stare out the window, contemplating my mortality. Good. That's right. I said it. Good. Finally done with this. All of this. These meaningless moments masquerading as life. Good. Time to move on. The wife and kids will be happy, eventually. Immediately? The money will come in handy. Well, what's left after the IRS taxes it, and my bad debts are paid, and then the IRS comes again. Better off, nonetheless.

The sweat starts to bead on my forehead. I can hear voices in the hallway. No, real voices. Doctor and nurse voices. Talking about . . . me. I crane my head to listen. Desperately clutching to my last moments here on earth. I want to know everything. See everything. Feel everything. Before I go. The door creaks open. There are several people in the hallway behind Dr. Lawrence. Their somber faces tell it all. Goner. Surprisingly, my eyes well with tears. OK, not surprisingly. I turn my head so he can't see. Weak me. Thin-skinned Earl. Never made his mommy happy. Now he's gonna be dead.

Dr. Lawrence's mouth is moving, but I can't hear. I'm thinking of how tonight's dinner will go with my family. The kids will be distraught. Wifey will be in disbelief. I will rise from the table majestically and . . . Wait, what? Panic attack? Waves of sound crash into my ears. *Panic attack!* Are you fucking kidding me? Panic attack? *Panic attack?* That doesn't even sound right. Like I can feel my chest tightening and my heart exploding and my breath shortening. But I guess you're the expert, "Doctor." If I die, this is all your fault.

So, I'm good? I mean, something has to be wrong, right? You can't just be having panic attacks. People don't just go around half dying and shit, and then they get some zit pads strapped to their tits and are told they are fucking fine. That is not the fucking narrative I want to spin past my family at dinner. No cancer, no heart disease, not even the goddamned flu. This is ridiculous. Fuck this. I'm not OK. I can't be OK. I have to be dying. Have to be. Well, if I'm OK, you won't mind me snorting a little coke in your parking lot, will you? Since I'm so fucking "OK." *Sniiiiifff*. Ahh! Yeah, how's that for OK, huh? Who's OK now, motherfucker? And if I'm back here lying on your goddamned table next month, don't blame me, jackass!

They never do.

6

LOCUST AVENUE

I had known Cameron Wilson a long time. He and his wife, Crystal, looked up to my parents. They adopted them as mentors. Cameron and Crystal were from Jamaica, and my mom had taken Crystal under her wing after she started working for us. Crystal was bright and ambitious. She reminded my mom of herself. They had two children and worked hard. Crystal learned the business the same way my mom did. She started at the very bottom. She worked as a housekeeper and a direct-care staff person and then slowly moved into medications and administration.

Back then, we could have one person handle the entire building of thirty-nine residents. This enabled my parents to make a ton of money by saving on salary expenses. Jamaicans seemed to be the only ones able to physically handle the job, however. Poverty in Jamaica ain't like poverty in America. Poverty here is living in an apartment with government-subsidized rent, food, and education. Poverty in Jamaica is no electricity, no running water, wondering where your next meal is coming from, and living in a one-room tin shed and dropping out of school at ten to work. That difference, that desperation, forges a steel in the character of those who are able to get here. They have a want that can only be grown from abject poverty. Island poverty. Real poverty. They have a want that isn't born here. Trust me on this one. I have seen that steel up close.

Crystal worked her way up in our company, and in many respects, she was part of the family. Their family would come by my mom's house and swim in the pool and eat dinner, attend the parties, and mingle with all the fake fuckers who smiled in my mom's face and secretly hated her for her success. Crystal even went out on her own and passed the state licensing exam to become an administrator. The property my family owned at Locust Avenue was vacant, and my mom and Crystal hammered out a deal to lease/purchase the property. Immediately, Crystal and Cameron went to work renovating. Cameron was a very handy guy. He could fix just about anything. He was a short, stumpy man with calloused hands. They were calloused by years of fighting starvation and manual labor, clawing his way to America—working at the airport and a factory. They were ready for this. Now, he spent his off time building their dream business: a residential care facility just like my mom and dad.

In exchange for the lack of a down payment on the building, Cameron performed maintenance duties for my parents. My father gave him a corporate Home Depot credit card, on which Cameron promptly ran up a mysterious $5,000 bill. He never explained why or what he did with those purchases. Even though it was clear they had been robbed, my parents' admiration for Crystal was so great and their desire to get the rent rolling in so deep, they looked the other way. When Cameron began to accumulate trucks and large machinery at the property—that were obviously stolen from his warehouse and airport jobs—my parents also overlooked it. They overlooked it because the building was taking shape. The rooms and kitchen and bathrooms were put together, the office was furnished, and the tile floors sparkled like Vatican glass. Crystal was going to be great, and the money was going to be rolling in. So they overlooked a lot. Unfortunately, they did not, however, overlook Leneeta.

The world takes all kinds of people to make it go 'round. In my business, you get used to the different idiosyncrasies of those who pretend to be sane. I laugh silently at us all feigning veils of normalcy except Leneeta.

Leneeta was clearly nuts.

I could see it from the jump. She walked into my mother's office with her crossed eyes and disheveled wig. She was too eager. She praised my parents continuously, but more than that, she was full of fucking shit. Supposedly, she was the heir to a real estate fortune in Florida. Her father had amassed millions of dollars in Florida apartments, and she was paid $70K per month to live on. She just wanted to invest that money and thought that this business was the ticket. OK, let me get this straight. You receive $70K per month to live on and have real estate holdings in a tropical climate, but you want to work in the section of a Northeastern city, affectionately known as "the bottom," with mentally disturbed people, fighting the State for licensing every year? Bullshit. My mother wanted to believe her. Leneeta sold her a dream, and the deal was done. Cameron and Crystal were out, and Leneeta was in. Cameron and Crystal were paid $10K for all the work they put into Locust Avenue. All the repairs and vases and paintings and signs and immaculately waxed floors were turned over to Leneeta's crazy fucking ass. I knew it wouldn't turn out well. I knew Leneeta was crazy. I hired Crystal to run Argyle Street, and Cameron went to work in a day care providing maintenance.

Years later, it all came to a head. Leneeta wasn't paying her mortgage to us. Eviction proceedings were underway. My phone had five missed calls from Crystal when I came out of the shower. I called her back, and she answered with "Turn on the channel six news." I did. There was Leneeta with her now-matted wig cocked to the side, ratty fur falling off her rail-thin shoulders being led out of Locust Avenue with her head hung in shame and her wrists locked in handcuffs. The reports flooded in. Locust Avenue had deteriorated into a house of horrors.

I stopped at the mechanic around the corner from Argyle Street to have my radiator looked at. For some reason, I decided to open the radiator cap myself. The steam seared the skin off my forearm as my phone rang. My morning was in chaos. So was my life. Thanks to the rampant inaccuracies in our city's recording office, reporters thought I was the owner of Locust Avenue and had descended on the poor mentally ill residents. My staff was warning me to stay away. The reporters apparently were literally hiding in the bushes.

After acquiring Locust Avenue, Leneeta had promptly become hooked on prescription medicine, which was convenient because she now had access to all the residents' meds. At least, I assume it was after, but who knows? The meds that she didn't ingest herself were sold to local fiends by her husband and son. To increase profits, she neglected to report to Social Security when clients died and continued to cash their checks. Clients died there often due to the neglect of their medical needs and their dietary restrictions and quite possibly their earnest desire to get the fuck away from Leneeta. Leneeta only fed them soup twice per day, every day. The home had also acquired a number of stray cats. The flea problem inside was reportedly so bad that some of the walls were black. Several toilets were broken yet continued to be used, which led to what some might call a slightly malodorous environment. Clients were being led out into daylight looking like survivors of the Middle Passage.

Over time, Leneeta's behavior became increasingly erratic. Testimony depicted a paranoid homeless-like existence for her. Physicians increasingly called me to question whether I still had anything to do with the building. When it was confirmed that I did not, the disappointment was palpable. No easy solution, huh, Doc? Leneeta's husband was a large, sweaty, bearded buffoon who many (including myself) mistook for a resident. With a proclivity for crime and a lack of intelligence, it surprised no one when he ended up in Albert Einstein Medical with three gunshots to his abdomen. Three masked men had robbed their row home in Germantown. Seventy thousand dollars per month, but you live in a Germantown row home. Keepin' it real . . . I guess? He claimed he saw nothing. This, of course, was the code of the streets. No snitching. He would deal with it himself. Unfortunately, he would never get the chance. He would never leave that hospital bed. Leneeta quickly descended into madness thereafter. Whatever semblance of a human being she had ever been died along with her husband. We should have known. We should have seen it coming.

The police officers removed their respirators. The

reporters' cameras flashed, and microphones assailed faces of nosy neighbors with less information than questions. These men of honor and strength did their absolute best to describe the scene inside, yet their words failed to truly embody the cruelty with which these people had been treated. It was more than just Leneeta. It was all of us. We allowed them to be lost from our thoughts. We didn't care. I was growing tired of this narrative. Certainly, that was not how it was going to be portrayed, but that is the truth. We don't care. We selfishly want these people to live just to make us feel better. But define "living." The officers could only thank that anonymous "hero" who had alerted DPW to the horror behind those walls. That anonymous caller had set those people free and reunited some of them with their families, who they had been prevented from seeing—literally saving some of their lives. Social Security launched an investigation, along with the FBI and DPW.

I watched Leneeta's news clippings with great interest. She wasn't charged with criminal neglect or client abuse or even narcotics trafficking. In the end, it was the one thing that really matters. The one thing you just don't fucking fuck with. Forget human lives. Forget common decency to your fellow human being. Money is what matters most. Uncle Sam's money, to be exact. She was charged with cashing several deceased residents' checks and sentenced to pay it back. Yep. No firing squad. No jail time. Not even a thousand lashes. Nothing. We know about all those lives destroyed, but we will forget about that. Just pay us back the $75K, and you can walk. OK, $35K and we cool.

Months earlier, I had paid a visit to Leneeta to try and help my parents collect the mortgage payments that she had missed. My parents were acting as the bank for her. For some odd reason, it didn't raise any red flags to Earl and Jackie when a woman with real estate holdings and a $70K per month passive income couldn't secure a mortgage. I guess we believe what we want. Once again, she handed me a check that both of us knew she couldn't cover. I stood in her office with the thin, filthy cot in the corner and a Harley Davidson motorcycle in the middle as she sat chain-smoking Newports and eating gray meatballs. I left and convinced my parents to start foreclosure procedures. They did, but it wouldn't be a quick process. She disgusted me. I hated her. I didn't care that her husband was dead. I didn't care that she was crazy. In her, I saw my future, and I hated what I saw.

God, I'm glad I fucking called in that anonymous tip.

7

SATURDAY

My kindergarten teacher gathered us all onto the mat in a circle. I was nervous because I didn't know anybody. I suppose nobody really knew anybody, but I'm positive I didn't know *anybody*. Little scared black boy from Mount Airy. So unsure of myself. So scared of life. I couldn't breathe. The morning ritual of telling about one's weekend had begun, and it was my first day at my new private school. Before we were to begin, our teacher decided to ask all of us in the group some questions. She had on a tight green sweater with an ornate pin. I always wondered if those pins hurt. Like how did they work? What did they mean? They looked like diamonds to me. Everything looked like diamonds to me, here. The kids were golden blond and white. Very white. Their smiles and shirts were very, very white. Painfully white. Exhaustingly white.

The group question was probably designed to break the ice, so to speak. Ya know, don't have one kid answering all by himself right away. She asked us questions like "What do you do before you cross the street?" We all answered in unison: "Look both ways!" She asked us, "What color is the sky?" We answered, "Blue!" Then she asked a question with an answer that would haunt me for years to come. She asked us, "What day do we go to church?" All the little smiling children except me, black and white alike, raised their confident voices in unison with a resounding "*Sunday!*" I was shocked and hoped nobody had heard me say Saturday.

Sunday? Da fuck?

Righteous indignation stems from one's fear of what one really is. The religious in our society wallow in their condemnation of others. They are comfortable condemning the unbaptized to hell or calling other groups "cults" or frowning upon the dogmatic practice of some other collection of fools. The truth of the matter is we are all crazy. Isn't it insane to sit Sunday after Sunday (or Saturday), staring blankly back at a man reading from a book that was supposedly written eons ago and interpreted centuries ago but printed three years ago, and we question nothing? I watched a documentary on Scientology. I don't know if what I saw was true because I am not a Scientologist, and I don't know any. However, what struck me was their utter belief in something that not only had I never heard of before but was also so superlatively different from anything I believed.

And they *believed*. With every fiber of their atomic biologically neurotic existence, they believed. They believed everything they were told, and that is something I have never been able to do. I am envious of the faithful. My mind just doesn't work that way. If you present something to me, I immediately question it. I have been a skeptic since day one. I question everything. Everything. Myself mostly. We don't all believe the same thing, but mass media is our national religion. It scares me how desperately we feel the need to "connect." Millions of Americans spend countless hours reading tweets and Instagram posts and status updates and bullshit. Man's base nature is to conform. Those doomed to spend a lifetime on the other side of the hill looking at the sheeple wondering what the fuck is going on are rare. Rare and alone.

Anyway, the point is I didn't know I was a Seventh-day Adventist until I was in that kindergarten class. I guess nobody thinks of themselves as anything but who they are until someone drops a label on they ass. We don't inherently think of ourselves as "that group" when we are immersed in that group because everyone is of that group as far as we are concerned. We all think that everyone is what we are. All I knew was that I hated getting up on Saturday mornings to attend church. I guess I should have been equally shocked that there were no Jewish kids there, but our view of the world is a selfish one, now, isn't it?

I recall pretending to be asleep or sick in order to avoid church at a very young age. Maybe this should have been a sign, but my mother kept plugging away. I never dug the scene. The preacher would stand in the pulpit in all these fancy robes and blabber on incoherently, and all these people would just accept whatever he said. Why were his interpretations accepted as fact? Why was he the only one allowed to speak? Why was I the only one with questions?

The adults just sat there in their pews staring blankly and accepting whatever came out of his mouth. I was too curious for that. The stories were too fantastic for that. The burning bush was talking, and the Red Sea was parting, and I wasn't fucking buying any of it. So one day I asked God if he was real. I was coming out of the science building on campus, and I stopped and stared up at the beautiful blue sky. Birds staring down at me innocently. Clouds floating lazily in the sky. My jacket was too tight and my corduroys too short. They always were. I asked God to show me a sign. I asked for a dead pigeon to be dropped at my feet. I waited in fear. I didn't believe there was a God, but man, what if I was wrong, and a dead pigeon dropped right out of the sky at my feet? How would I explain that turn of events? I nervously scanned the sky for incoming deceased fowl, but none did appear that day. For me it served as confirmation, but looking back, it was foolish. Even if there was a God, why would he take the time to show me his awesome power? Me. A malcontent. A heathen. Too lazy to even get up and worship. On Saturday.

I believe there is an energy we all share. There is a power that is in us and around us. You can call it "God" or whatever you want. Energy can neither be created nor destroyed. Therefore, it always has been and always will be; it just changes form. So we are all God, and we are all powerful. The dogma they feed us is just designed to confuse and control us. It only serves to divide and conquer us. Maybe the residents are onto something. Maybe they have tapped deep into that power, and it has released them from the base desires and confines of our normal existence. Maybe those voices are a manifestation of energy that has changed form and is trying to contact us all. Maybe we perceive them as crazy, but they are the ones that are sane. They eat, sleep, fuck, shit, and die and don't care what anyone thinks about how they look or smell or talk or if they go to church on Saturday.

8

THE TRUTH ABOUT TRUST

Why perform tests on animals when we have pedophiles in prison?

-Anonymous

Every so often, the monotony that is my life is interrupted. Actually, this happens every day, but these interruptions become the monotony. Sucks to be me. My business is open 24-7-365, and my employees all believe that I am allergic to sleep. Well, now I am, but accessing me regularly was never a worry for them since they sensed I was a vampire. So it comes as no surprise when my phone rings at seven thirty one morning, and it's my administrator, Crystal Wilson. She is upset. I am upset because my sleep has been broken. I will never be able to sleep late again. This phone call will forever change the course of my life and my thinking and, eventually, my entire view of the world.

After losing Locust Avenue to Leneeta, Crystal had come to work with me. She was an awesome employee. It is rare in our business to find someone who is both smart and hardworking at the right price. I suppose that is rare in any business, really. She had an administrator's license, and she was well versed in the direct-care portion of the business as well, having worked her way up in my mother's company years earlier. This enabled her to handle the office and all the administrative duties while at the same time filling a shift as a direct-care provider and enabled me to move far away from the business and save some money to boot. However, all that glitters isn't gold, and I would soon see firsthand how quickly the tide can change in life.

She didn't sound irritated or angry on the phone; she sounded scared really. I guess my assumption of irritation was due to the nature of our business. Our business requires everything to be reported. It doesn't matter how trivial or ridiculous that incident is; we must report it. Mrs. Schitz was our new director of DPW, and she ran the department the same way Hitler ran the Third Reich. Fear permeated every phone call and knock at the door. Every decision we made was predicated upon what we thought Mrs. Schitz might think or send the gestapo cyborgs to do to us. She had recently successfully closed over two hundred homes in the city of Philadelphia alone. Two hundred homes. Three thousand beds. Closed. So Crystal's lack of irritation but strong sense of fear was not alarming . . . yet.

Crystal had been stellar, so when she suggested her husband come work part time for us, I quickly said yes. Cameron was one of those men who could do it all but couldn't seem to put his life together. I fear we had a kinship in that respect. I am usually able to put my finger on exactly what someone's fatal flaw is. Normally it's stupidity, but Cameron wasn't stupid. There was something holding him back, but that something was benefitting me, so maybe that's why I never dwelled upon it.

Crystal told me there had been an accusation against Cameron. One of our residents had accused him of rape. Jesus. This was the biggie. Well, I guess the biggie is murder, but fuck, this might as well be murder. This was crazy. My mind was spinning. Did she just say rape? Yep. She said rape. Good lord! I'm . . . fainting. My deceased brother, Marcus, appeared and turned his head toward me and stared. Eyes wide and sunken. Lips black. His once beautiful skin ashen. I didn't faint. I focused.

Ignorance is not knowing. I—in my ignorance as to what rape is really about—immediately had my doubts. Cameron? A married man and deacon of the church with two children would rape Erin, a mentally disabled burn victim? When I say burn victim, I mean *burn* victim. Erin was . . . how do I say? . . . less than aesthetically pleasing to the eye. OK, fuck it. She was ugly. And she had a lisp. Her skin melted into itself and scarred horrifically. She was legally blind and obese. She slurred her words, and spittle whizzed past your head like bullets in a war zone during any conversation. Neo-esque maneuvers were required to avoid being hit. That was my ignorance. Rape isn't about attraction as much as it is about control. It's about dominating another human being. You never really know what's going on inside another person's head, and a psychopath is especially hard to comprehend. They rape to dominate. To them, rape is the ultimate expression of violence and anger toward their victim. Some rapists fetishize violence, so then rape is a sexual satisfaction as well. I will never understand it.

I had to hustle my ass into the office and perform an investigation. I thought this was, of course, ridiculous. Surely this was a mistake, or maybe Erin had it in for Cameron. I had witnessed Erin "flirting" with other residents and the jealousy this created in her husband, Leland. Maybe Leland thought Erin and Cameron had something going on, so he made her do this? Maybe she was so blind she thought Cameron did this, and really another resident had done it?

Maybe.

Maybe.

Maybe.

Erin stuck to her guns.

Most of my job entails putting out a lot of fires. The

most important part of that process is always pretending that the fire isn't quite as big as it is. It's like when the doctor first sees you in the emergency room, she can't say, "Holy fucking shit, how did that get in your fucking asshole?" Instead she has to say, "OK, Mr. So-and-So, what seems to be the problem?" Speaking of which, I once had to convince Frank that snakes and mice couldn't crawl up his ass without him knowing. No, Frank, I think you are definitely gonna feel that one . . . but I digress.

My staff looks to me just as much as the residents do in this regard. When I walk through the door, I have to enter with confidence. I must maintain an air of "Everything is fucking all right, people! I am here. I know everything. Chill the fuck out and fuck that shit. I got this!"

It was hard, but I did it. Leland and Erin were summoned to my subterranean office. The same office my mother had occupied. The same desk my mother had sat at so many years ago. She built this business with moxie and blood and sweat and tears, and I wasn't going to let these motherfuckers destroy it!. Ahem. "Please have a seat, Erin."

When questioned by DPW, I categorically denied being biased. I pretended to be appalled at the suggestion. I'm a great fucking actor, but Erin felt it right away. Truth be told, I did grill her. Truth be told, I didn't believe her. Truth be told, I was defensive of Cameron and my business and, I guess, in many ways of myself. What did it say about me that I employed a sexual predator? That I trusted a person like that? Not much. I was ashamed. Erin sat shyly smiling in my office while her husband (who also lived there) maneuvered his six-foot-five-inch frame down the narrow staircase and through the door.

Leland and Erin had met at the psych program over ten years ago. Maybe it was the apple juice and crackers or the way she drooled while coloring—we may never know—but a love story was born. They had both lived in personal care homes at the time and were seeking a home that would allow them to move in together. No problem. They were an easygoing couple for the most part. They required their meds to be monitored, and they needed hygiene prompting, but nothing too wild for our business. Every so often, Leland would yearn for independence. Once, he had his case manager get him a job stocking shelves at Pathmark. He lasted two weeks. He had several increasingly psychotic episodes in the store, including screaming at the top of his lungs while hurling canned goods through the aisles. Apparently not too good for business. His case manager apologized yet vowed to get him another job. It's just fucked up the way the government does them. The problem is that the government sends them only eighty-five bucks per month for a spending allowance. If they want to earn more money, they have to get a job, but they have to deduct the money they earn off their check. The government doesn't want them to reenter society. It fosters their dependence on the system. Granted, most of them are fucked beyond belief, but for the few who may have some sense, what hope do they have to ever become independent?

They told me their story. Leland sat there with this weird confidence I had never seen before. He had the air of a father demanding his daughter tell the principal what happened at recess. His arms were folded and his chin craned upward to the right. He looked regal despite his wrinkled clothes and the oatmeal that had crusted on his mouth. He looked down on us while Erin did her best to tell the story.

She remembered how Leland had been hospitalized for a psychotic episode for a week and how Cameron would work the overnight shift. This all must have happened when I moved to Georgia because I had no idea what the fuck she was talking about. I had gone to great lengths to escape the business, but the goddamned housing market dragged me back. Fucking Lehman Brothers. I remained cool and calm. Cameron had been cleaning her floor late at night when he came into her room and slid into bed with her. She had her back to the door and was slightly asleep. He removed her panties and slid his penis into her and raped her. Not kind of raped her. Raped her raped her. She giggled while she told me this. Giggled? I didn't believe it. I mean, these people have serious psychiatric issues. This should have been my exit, but sadly, it wasn't. When they left me alone, I began to hyperventilate. My emotions spanned from anger to disappointment to fear. What was

going to happen to my business? This wasn't greed, people
—OK, maybe a little—but fuck, I had two small children, a
wife, and no discernible skills. What would I do without
this shit?

I went home that night and relayed the story to my wife.
Neither one of us believed this story. Looking back, our
ignorance was astounding. It's easy to have perspective
when events are far removed both chronologically and
emotionally. Like on television when they say, "He always
seemed like such a nice guy." In the moment, the comfort of
ignorance surrounds you, and you lie back, kick up your
feet, and wallow in it. Though I had no doubt this was a
false story, I had the loathsome responsibility of reporting
the incident to DPW. The law stated that I had twenty-four
hours after an incident to report that incident. I intended to
use every minute.

I sat in my bed not resting. Not sleeping. Eyes wide
open. Mind racing. Talking myself through all the scenarios.
How could I legally not report and save Cameron from the
shame he would face? Save my business from the scrutiny?
Shut Erin up? I could think of nothing. I was fucked.

Daylight knifed through the shades. My wife lay sound
asleep. I slipped out of bed and descended the stairs to my
office. I stared at the incident report I had filled out the
previous day. Stared at the word *rape* until it meant nothing.
Until it got blurry. Until it dissolved into the paper. But it
just wouldn't go away.

The tears began to stream down my face as I pressed send on the fax machine. I was ruining a man's life. A good man's life. All because of these stupid rules and regulations and dotted *i*'s and crossed *t*'s. I knew what was happening in my home. I knew what kind of people these residents were. I didn't need the State poking their noses around, telling me what was what and who was who. Besides, all they would do was come in and find violations on me.

I called the cops when I got to the office. It took them three days to come out and investigate. Three days. I found solace in their dismissiveness. Detective Henry looked bored. His shoes were hush puppies with the large rubber lip built for function over fashion, and his suit was dull brown to match his fading blue shirt and capacity for concern. He asked routine questions to my staff and myself and the victim. He took Cameron's info, and he left. I had been holding my breath in anticipation of their fury. My guilt at having allowed this to occur was stressing me considerably. It undermined my sobriety, and I tumbled down into my addiction again.

That's me sitting in the parked car behind LA Fitness by the dumpster. Snorting cocaine. Hands trembling. Stomach turning. Paranoid. In my rearview mirror, Marcus stares at me. The tendons and muscles in his neck strain against his skin. He was so thin. I leave and go back to bed. Eat something; you will feel better. I felt a large weight lifting from my back. I could breathe again.

Then the State showed up.

I hate the State. I hate their righteous indignation. I hate their condescension. I hate their lunch breaks and their youth and their maturity and their delusional expertise. I hate them. These assholes who deem it fit to pay me thirty-four dollars a day to care for a human being have the gall to stride into my building and take me hostage for two days while they invade my office and my files and my life and try to determine exactly how this is my fault or how I somehow could have predicted that a rape would have occurred or that noting Erin's burn scars on her support plan might have preventative qualities. *Ahh!*

They commandeered my office and set up camp. They demanded the files of all employees on shift within twenty-four hours of the incident. Which, by the way, had occurred four years earlier. Oh yeah, I forgot to mention that. Erin neglected to report this rape for four fucking years apparently. Wait, what? Why? She couldn't remember exactly when it occurred and had continued to live there for four more years with Cameron working there. Yeah, sounds reasonable. I didn't know. Rape is strange. Must be hard to deal with. You rape me, and I'm telling, motherfucker. Right away. Telling, telling, telling. Hey, everybody, listen up! That motherfucker raped me!

Anyway, the three motherfuckers from the state poured over the employee files. They then took a lunch break . . . in my office. Schruter was the ringleader. She packed her lunch in plastic tubs labeled "sandwich" (in case she forgot?) and carried a recyclable bag. Her cronies were forced to follow suit. Who has the temerity to eat lunch in someone else's office? After offending my polite sensibilities, not to mention my nostrils, they laid into Erin's file and Leland's file. They asked me to leave my office so that they could confer. Yes, I left. It was hard to hold my tongue. Hard to hold my fist. Hard to hold my tears, but I left.

I remembered how, months earlier, our resident Leo had flooded the building overnight. Leo's one of my favorite residents. He has the mind of a three-year-old and the heart of an angel. One evening, he decided to take a "steam shower." He opened the shower curtain and turned the spigot outward into the bathroom. The hot water poured all over the floor while the bathroom filled with steam. Leo stood in the middle naked to allow his skin to moisturize for an hour. Seems reasonable enough, right? Water is an opportunistic enemy; it found its way through the nooks and crannies of my sixty-year-old building to the first floor. It decimated ceiling tiles and electrical wiring all along its path. Three a.m. I was called and forced out of my bed to handle the situation. After securing an emergency electrician to ensure our residents' safety, I directed a cleanup of the disaster and returned to my bed for a couple of hours of rest. At 8:00 a.m., I was back up and inside Home Depot buying ceiling tiles and renting a carpet-cleaning machine when my phone rang once again. The State was in my building. I didn't panic. Shit, I was proud of how I handled the situation. Inspector Dullard wanted to know where I was, so I assured him that he wasn't my wife but that I was at Home Depot. When I arrived back at Argyle Street, I spoke to Inspector Dullard briefly before I set to cutting tiles and replacing them. He didn't ask me about the damage, and I thought it was self-explanatory.

At the end of his inspection, he informed me that I would be receiving a violation for 85A . . . unsanitary conditions. The law states that missing ceiling tiles are unsanitary conditions. That's fucking insane! How quickly must one replace the tiles to avoid a violation? On top of that, I was facing a fine. Three hundred dollars per client per day because I had received an 85A on my last inspection. 85A. Unsanitary conditions. That's some bullshit. They put that bullshit on the website too. The last time was for an uncovered wastebasket in a bathroom. Fuck you, Dullard. *Fuck. You.* It took all my inner strength not to strangle him. I envisioned his eyes bulging while I squeezed his esophagus with my soot-covered hands. I could see the life leaving his body and feel the joy increasing in mine as it did . . . I dropped the X-Acto knife, left him there in the hallway, and went to breakfast. Fuck it. That same feeling came over me that morning, but I stayed calm.

They summoned me back into my office. Their somber faces foreshadowed the ass fucking they were going to perform on me. Strap me down to my desk one crony on each side while old woman Schuter rammed that PA5500 up my ass. It doesn't matter what they found. Truth is, I can't remember what they found, but I'm pretty sure that nowhere in my instructions to staff did it say, "Rape Erin." They never left my office. They spent five hours at my building poring over files. Determined to lay the blame at my feet. They spent thirty-five minutes talking to Erin. Thirty-five fucking minutes talking to the actual victim. That's all they deemed worthy. It was clear to me what their objective was. Let's pin this on the owner. Let's fry him. He's a dirty, thieving provider.

When it was all said and done, they instructed me that I should have called an independent investigator because I wasn't qualified to investigate a rape. *No shit, bitch. That's why I called the fucking cops.* They then blamed me for the cops taking three days to get to the building. They gave me several violations for procedural mishaps, wagged their fingers, and departed my office feeling as though they had once again protected the mentally disabled from the bad, bad provider. Fucking makes me sick.

The cops didn't press charges because Erin didn't want to. In fact, she stated that she liked Cameron and wanted him to keep working there because he was "the nicest employee we have." Nice . . . except for the rape thing, I guess. Cameron never set foot in my building again.

Unfortunately, his saga was just beginning.

Five months later, I get another phone call from Crystal.

My after-coke-binge sleep was rudely interrupted. This time she was upset. She was crying. She was bawling. I could barely make out what she was saying. Cameron had been arrested. For child molestation. Seven girls from his church —including Crystal's own sister—had accused him of molesting them over the past ten years. They had gained courage by watching the Penn State-Jerry Sandusky case unfold, and when they came forward, it was a shocker. The youngest had been eight years old when it started. Rumor had it that Crystal's nephew was his son. I watched the news reports and read the paper daily following the drama.

Apparently, Cameron had been a known sexual predator since before he came to the States from Jamaica. He had fled to our country to avoid the Caribbean justice (the business end of a machete) he faced for molesting a physically disabled woman. Here, he had preyed on the youth of his church, using his position as deacon and youth minister. The girls recounted the horrors of being taken to cheap motel rooms in the church van and raped. Can you imagine? The deacon of the fucking church, volunteering to drive those kids and preying on those kids? Imagine the fear those girls had. Fear that gripped them and closed their mouths. He raped one girl at a sleepover for his daughter. Took her to another room while his own child lay asleep only a few feet away. My mind was blown. Cameron *was* a rapist. He *had* raped Erin. He was a monster.

Monsters live among us.

These sexual predators are something else. They are an aberrational natural phenomena. I thought about *Push,*the book about that girl Precious. The book is much more sickening than the movie, by the way. Precious describes being molested by her father and her mixed-up emotions. How she was being raped, but, physically, her body reacted like she was having consensual sex. How her vaginal juices were "popping like fried chicken grease" as he fucked her from behind. Disgusting. I read everything I could about these monsters, trying to understand how someone I had known for that long could be like . . . that. Someone who had been to my family barbecues, swam in my family pool. Met my kids. They are narcissists. They are manipulators. They cannot be rehabilitated. The boogeyman is real. My world was not.

The church elders had known for years. Instead of turning him in, they performed an anointing ritual on him. Washing him in holy water would do the trick, right? White robes and holy water. I wish someone had informed me of their thinking. They might have mentioned that when I called for references. "Works well with others, always on time, rapes children, quick learner."

It was surreal to me. My saving grace was that, thankfully, through all the questioning, Cameron had spared me the embarrassment of revealing his previous place of employment. Maybe the cops were embarrassed as well, seeing as they had not found it prudent to prosecute him earlier because they never mentioned the Erin situation either. He got forty years in prison when it was all said and done. Crystal couldn't face the world and quit. Me? I got up, got dressed, and went to work. Because that's what we do, right? We work. We live. We fuck. We hurt. We die. Every day just melts into the next. Of course, mine were beginning to fray at the seams, coated by a fine white powder at each tear.

9

NIGHTMARES

F ear is paralyzing, all encompassing, and the only thing that is real. We share its presence and must overcome it. My dreams are all about fear. Shit, my awake state is all about fear. In my dreams, I am walking through my childhood home. No, not the mansion on Sedgwick with the game room and the pool and the six bedrooms. No. The one on Allens Lane. The tiny one. The one I went to visit with my wife.

It had been years, and I happened to be in the market for a classic car. An ad in the paper for a 1960 Buick Regal caught my eye. The white beast was parked on Stenton Avenue. Rotting. Neglected. The phone was answered by an irritated man. I could hear his wife in the background, yelling about some bullshit. It's all bullshit. The dirty dishes, the unmade bed, the cluttered garage. All bullshit. I heard myself asking about visiting the house. I heard me being surprised he lived in the house I grew up in. That he had purchased it from my parents. I could remember the little table in my room that housed my Matchbox cars and the single bathroom we had in the hallway. Maybe that's why I hate houses with one bathroom now. Maybe that's why my bladder is weak now. Holding my piss for what felt like hours. Wriggling around in my bed, hoping whoever was in the bathroom would finally be done.

In my dream, I head into the kitchen, and the dishes are piled in the sink, and that fruit-and-vegetables wallpaper has the dimples in it, and there I see the phone number I wrote on the wall, and I am being pulled to the stairs. They are so dark. I step out into the darkness, and I'm falling. My heart is racing, and I'm sweating and screaming, but no sound emits from me. Right before I hit the ground, my eyes erupt open. I gasp. I'm looking around. Where am I? Where are any of us? I'm fucking living in a Talking Heads video. I swear all of what I see around me is just a play for my eyes only. Maybe I'm still asleep.

I'm five years old in the kitchen again. My dad just came home from work. My hero just came home from work. Only thing I love more than him is my piece of green felt blanket. Took me ten years to realize my mom had given me a scrap of felt after she made a tablecloth for the table. Took me even longer to realize we were poor. Generic food labels. Shopping at the thrift store. Never gave me a clue. Pops walks in. I love his uniform. I love his gun and his belt. And his beard. He looms over me. Smiling. Tired. Pops is a park ranger. Assistant supervisor in charge of protection. To me, he is the coolest motherfucker on the planet. He has perfectly creased forest-green pants. There are three pleats in the back of his shirt. Never figured out how he did that. Three pleats. I grab his hat off the table and place it on my head while running around the kitchen. I beam up at him and tell him that one day I am going to be a park ranger. His face changes. He doesn't look angry just . . . changed. Looking deeply into my eyes, he pleads with me to promise him one thing in life. "Please don't be a park ranger." Maybe that's where I lost it. I never really had a conviction to be anything after that. I had been convinced that that was the pinnacle of existence. I mean, who wouldn't want to be a park ranger? He got to have a gun and hang in the park and got an office in a big tower near the Liberty Bell and take private tours of the historical monuments. Did I mention he got to carry a gun?

"Please don't be a park ranger."

"Please don't be me." Is that what he meant? Do all fathers look at their lives at some point and hope desperately that no one they create repeats it? I do. Guess I made you proud, Dad. I didn't become a park ranger. As a matter of fact, I didn't become anything at all.

10

RAW

The woman at the front desk pretended not to see me struggling to open the front door. Their Ring Buzzer sign had long fallen off, but she was determined to make that my problem. I finally located it, and she responded via the intercom: "May I help you?" Yes, you *can* help me. You're the front desk lady, ain't ya? You can stop being such a fucking cunt and open the fucking door. I don't need directions to the goddamned IHOP.

I didn't say that, of course. I informed her I was here to see the patient Marcellus Mattox, and as I signed in, I mentally pulled a bow knife out and slit her throat. She bled out on the matted-down carpet, screaming for me to help. I peed on her head, then walked down the hall to Marcellus's room. I hadn't seen Marcellus in the three months since we sent him to the ER for breathing trouble. His daughter informed me in her passionately ghetto vernacular that Marcellus was fucked up. Despite her accurate description of the situation, I wasn't prepared. His skin or his lack thereof was . . . unnerving. Large swaths of skin had given way to raw, bloody tracks all over his body. He looked as though someone had attacked him with a potato peeler. What little hair he had previously possessed had abandoned him, and his frail frame had become emaciated to a degree that I am sure would be unacceptable even to the Third Reich.

I tried to hide the shock I felt. This abomination lay before me. I'm sure Marcellus noticed. The eyes cannot lie. There is that instant when you see something shocking, jarring, that the pupils dilate. It is an uncontrollable response of revulsion. I was revolted. Marcellus was revolting. Marcellus was suffering. He looked like he was dying. He looked like my brother, Marcus.

It's true we are all dying; however, his death looked a tad bit more imminent. Through his imminent death, peeling skin, and hair loss, Marcellus remained focused. He wanted his cigarettes and his eighty-five dollars per month. I often complain about the lack of funding the Commonwealth of Pennsylvania provides as it relates to providers. It is true that caring for a human being for thirty-four dollars a day is a crime. DHS/DPW should be prosecuted. They have willfully fought the raising of the state supplement, even though it has nothing to do with their budget needs and will only serve to provide a better living for the residents they are charged with protecting.

In 2000, the Commonwealth commissioned a sixty-page report that detailed the true cost of providing care and housing in the personal care industry, the benefit our business provided the community, the risks our population faced without our services, and the viability of our industry long term. At the time, we were receiving somewhere in the neighborhood of $900 per month, and they concluded we needed at least $1,800 per month. The report was submitted to DPW for commentary. Their commentary was short and sweet: "It is the department's opinion that the providers do not need an increase in pay."

And so we didn't get one. That simple. Fifteen years later, the state was still only paying $1,172.30 per month. Not quite $1,800, huh? That is egregious in and of itself, but maybe even more so is the personal-needs allowance for the residents: $85 per month. True, we as providers have the option to give them more, but does it make sense for me to charge even less than $34 a day? Regardless of the paltry amount (or maybe because of it), every resident desperately wants their 85 bucks. Marcellus was no different; never mind the fact that he had no fucking skin and shit.

His nurse was angry when she walked into the room.

She had been informed of my visit. "How y'all gonna send him looking like this to us?" She glared. *Pause.* In the immortal words of Dolemite, "Bitch, are you for real?" Was this the game we were going to play? Really. I mean not only is this a waste of time; it's insulting to my intelligence, and it's a thousand degrees outside, and I'm tired, and I hate you and my life and my business and Marcellus's skin . . . or lack thereof. The blame game is so boring and juvenile. Instead of finding solutions for this poor man, the rehab hospital was gearing up to defend the lawsuit his family would no doubt bring. Did they really believe I would forget that Marcellus had skin *before* he went to the hospital? We ain't talking glasses, lady. We talking skin. A motherfucker will remember if a motherfucker had skin or not. I guess it was worth a try.

I checked her hard and quick. Can't let some bullshit like that just slide. "Absolutely untrue. Mr. Mattox had all his skin intact when he was transported to the emergency room. Whatever reaction he is exhibiting now is a result of care and treatment or allergies he encountered thereafter . . . bitch." She was obviously sent to feel me out, intimidate the ignorant personal care provider with medical jargon and force me to admit culpability. Fuck outta here. After responding to her salvo of absurdity, I turned my attention to Marcellus and his potato-peeled skin.

He was a pitiful sight, sitting there all bandaged up. Not bandaged enough. Whining for his eighty-five dollars, and fuck me, I hadn't brought change. Not enough singles and fives for Master Mattox. He dispatched me to the 7-Eleven for change. I was happy to leave his presence. When I returned, the nurse was gone. Marcellus and I were alone. He looked so tired. He looked tired of living. He looked as though if he had the choice, he would smoke a pack, then lie down and never open his eyes again. I gotta remember to count my blessings. I was born with a semi- functioning brain and all my fingers and toes and whatnot. I hadn't ever been in a horrifically disfiguring accident. My kids were healthy. All the bullshit in my life existed through my own manifestations and viewpoint thereof. Marcellus had real problems. Shit, he didn't even have skin.s

His daughter kept me abreast of his condition and whereabouts through her ranting ghetto phone updates. Marcellus's skin hadn't cleared up over time; it was only worsening. She decided (for some weird, unknown reason) to check him out and drive him in her car to another hospital. I love you, Dad, but you can't ride in my car with no skin. He was taken into yet another hospital, where they examined him, performed tests, and conferred for days. They came up with the conclusion that his skin was fucked up. Well, that's not the technical term they used, but I got the ghetto report from Daddy's little girl, so that's what I know.

Lawsuits are common in my business. Once, while driving down a Georgia road (I moved to Georgia for four years trying to escape my business), I got a call from a family member of a recently deceased client. He began the conversation by saying, "Imma sue you."

I was in a terrible mood because my car once again needed service, so before I could catch myself, I barked back, "Who the fuck is this?" He went on to explain that while he had spent the last twenty years in prison and never called or written his mom (and I had been providing all her goddamned care), he was now out and going to sue me for the death of his ninety-three-year-old mom. "Hey, asshole, I didn't kill your mom. Time did. Go fuck yourself." Click. Point of fact, I didn't say that part. Fear.

An employee once sued us for injuries she claimed she received when at three o'clock in the afternoon, she slipped on a bag of frozen peas dropped by the food delivery truck that was in the driveway. "Couldn't walk around it, huh?" It just goes to show you what kind of asshole shit I was preparing myself for in this Mattox situation.

Every time the phone rang, I was jumpy. I was mentally preparing for the lawsuit. It doesn't matter if you're guilty or not. Trial lawyers sue everybody and let the defendants work it out. They work on a percentage-of-settlement basis, so while I'm going broke paying legal fees, the goddamned plaintiff is chilling. The theory is that the legal fees will reach critical mass, and the defendant or insurance company will deem it fiscally responsible to settle.

The lawsuit never came, and my life returned to the

normal humdrum of personal care administration: dealing with bullshit, paying the Johns, running errands, answering 3:00 a.m. phone calls, dancing in the hallway with residents, avoiding the office, lying to DPW, drinking booze to balance snorting cocaine, sleeping at my desk, crying in the shower, and so on and so on . . . until death do us part.

Curiosity overcame my better sensibilities one day. I hadn't heard from the ghetto reporter in months. Marcellus's money had accumulated a bit, but I noticed his direct deposit had slowed down to a trickle. I couldn't resist. Her terse ignorant answers were a welcome distraction from my routine. Marcellus was in a nursing home, bedridden. Skin still raw. I heard myself offering to drive the two and a half hours to his bedside to deliver his $170. Why would I do that? I can't really tell. Compassion. Fascination. Boredom. What attracts us to car crashes? Is it sympathy or sapidity? Marcellus was unrecognizable in his mummified state. He couldn't move his arms or legs and could barely talk, yet he managed to recount to me his nightly torture of bandage removal. Unable to heal, his wounds oozed into the bandages, and, when they were removed, they would peel another layer of skin from his body. The pain was excruciating. He had tears in his eyes looking up at me. Pleading with me to do . . . *something*.

I recalled the first time I had met him. His caseworkers had done a typically terrible job of describing his present condition. Fucking liars. Well, strike that. They actually did a great job. Their job was to lie to me, so I would say yes to admitting him sight unseen. I did. Fucking liars. Marcellus showed up looking aggressively homeless. His hair was matted, and he smelled like shit, mainly due to the shit that was encrusted in his underwear and jeans. The guy who created FUBU might be a billionaire, but his shitty clothing is worn by homeless people 'round the world. The once dark-blue denim FUBU jeans were black with soot and grease and shit and life and neglect and pain. We had him strip in the basement laundry room. He needed a lot of assistance. His hands were in a state of semi paralysis, and he shuffled when he walked. It looked as though his feet were stuttering. The tinkle on the floor caught everyone's attention. Crack pipe and crack rolled to my feet. Great. He's an addict to boot.

We cleaned Marcellus up that day. No need to wash his clothes; that's what incinerators are for. Destroyed his crack pipe and crack. He hadn't had a bath in a year because his house had become a crack den with no heat, electricity, or water. Drugs are jealous bitches. They don't want you doing anything else besides them.

We worked with Marcellus. We worked on his walk and his bowels and bladder and diet and health care and his addiction, and he got better. We dressed him in new clothes and encouraged a regular hygiene pattern and brought in therapists, and he got better. We took him on outings to Old

Country Buffet and the zoo and toured the city, and he got better.

And now here he was. His big brown eyes were staring up at me, welling up with tears because he knew he wasn't going to get better. He didn't want his $170. He didn't want any cigarettes. He wanted to talk. He wanted to know how everybody back at the building was doing. Was Nancy still ordering money? Was Brenda still screaming? Was Ricky still mean? His eyes kind of smiled as I told him how everyone was doing, and I lied to him, saying they all asked about him as well. Nobody had asked about him.

As my stories wound down, I could see the desperation in his eyes. The room was too cold, too dark, too solitary. Marcellus was scared, and he was alone. He had made a lot of bad choices in life, but at least he had choices back then. At least he had control. Now he was without a choice. Maybe the only thing that makes us human. He couldn't shuffle out of here and smoke some crack and die in a ditch. No, he was sentenced to nightly skin peeling, IV fluids, liquid diets, and a slow tedious descent into blackness. He didn't want to go. Not like that. I had to go. Just like that.

As I walked out of the room, he said, "Thank you, Earl." Fuck you, Marcellus. Fuck you, Marcellus! And fuck this goddamn fucking shit-ass business. We don't do shit! I didn't do shit but fuck up your life. Should have left you in the gutter to die high, filthy, ignorant,

and . . .

and . . .

and . . .

Happy.

God damn these fucking tears. You're welcome, man. Safe passage.

11

COCAINE

I am going to try to stop being a drug addict.

It's getting old. I'm getting old.

I don't want any applause or heartfelt praise for this decision because, frankly, I'm not making any promises. It's a goal of mine, like making it into the NFL was when I was fifteen years old. I'll give you one guess as to how that shit worked out. I guarantee you it wasn't from lack of trying. The fact is that this "sobriety" shit may not stick. To be perfectly honest, I've tried it before and changed my mind shortly thereafter. Anyway, this time I have a plan. Against my counselor's advice, I'm going to replace cocaine with coffee. I figure caffeine is close enough. But whaddaya know: coffee is fucking expensive. They charge like ten bucks for a fucking mocha and brownie at the Borders bookshop. *Ten fucking bucks!* All I'm thinking at the counter is *Do you know how much blow I could get for ten bucks?* Well, not much, but the point is that's the problem with addicts; we think of everything in terms of coke. Do you know how long I used to fuck on blow? Do you realize how much money I'm saving by not buying blow? See the way he wiped his nose after coming from the bathroom? He's doing blow. We fail to realize that nobody else measures their quality of life by the "coke-o-meter."

Life's become frustrating, and you nonaddicts are some fucking pricks. You look at me and say how sad: a bright young man throwing his life away on drugs. Fuck you. We're all on drugs. Everybody. If the government outlawed cigarettes tomorrow, my neighbor Pearl would be sucking dick on the corner of Peachtree and Pine to get a pack of Salem Light 100s. It's all about convenience. Convenience and lobbying. That's what it's about.

I need to get all my drug dealers together and form a political action committee. We'll call it DopePAC. We'll hire a research company to scientifically prove that cocaine and prostitution should be legal. We'll flood Congress with gobs of cash. I'll hold senators in my pocket like so many marbles. VICE will do an in-depth story on the benefits of a speedball. Bill Maher will light a joint on-air in support. I'll funnel cash from pimps to political analysts to seriously discuss the merits of twenty-four-hour brothels on morning news magazine shows. All the hustlers will turn into Washington insiders. It'll be fucking great, and I'll get rich because that's what it's really about. It's about getting rich. Rich enough to buy a mansion and an Aston Martin and coffee, lots of fucking coffee because I'm sober now, and coffee is fucking expensive.

Breathe. "Um, what did you say? . . . Yeah, venti, please."

My wife threw me a surprise party for my twenty-eighth birthday. I wasn't really surprised because Ray and Kenny, who were charged with keeping me out of the apartment for the day, are really terrible at stealth operations. They shuttled me around to random spots, all the while checking their watches and whispering into their phones. That's love. Dragging your friend around the filthy city of Philadelphia so his wife can decorate. Thanks, guys.

I was, however, surprised by the attendees. When we finally arrived back at the apartment, I opened the door to a deluge of nostalgia yelling *Surprise!* at me. Nyla, Nyla's future ex-husband, Brook, Brook's future ex-husband, et cetera, et cetera. It was beautiful and overwhelming at the same time. The most surprising was my main man, Colin (and his future ex-wife, Jen). Colin was a great friend and inspiration. He was a self-made man, an artist entrepreneur who created beautiful paintings of gangster rap in the early eighties and had been riding the wave for twenty-plus years.

As the music blared and the drinks flowed, Colin grabbed me and pulled me into my bedroom.

"You gotta do something."

"What the fuck are you talking about, Colin? I am doing something. I'm dancing and chillin'."

"No, some of this."

He proceeds to dump an entire pharmacy on my dresser. Blue pills and white pills and red pills oh my! And powder. "White girl." Yup, *my* soon-to-be ex-wife (well, I suppose soon is relative). I didn't know what the hell any of it was. All my life, I had been a drinker. Well, I did go through a weed phase in college, but when somebody slipped me a mickey and I ended up in a tranny's apartment in Baltimore, I had given that up. Anyway, Johnny Walker Black with two ice cubes was as far as I would go. Colin was adamant. I was hesitant. I surveyed my options. I chose cocaine. I will never be sure why I did it. I guess I thought it would be easy to do once and forget. People say once you try heroin, you are hooked, so I didn't want that. Pills were scary to me. Why coke wasn't scary . . . I still have no clue.

Colin returned his pills and whatnot to his pocket, leaving the little baggie on my dresser. My nerves were on edge. I didn't want someone to hear us or open the door or anything. He poured a tiny line out on the dresser and handed me a straw. I caught my reflection in the mirror as I leaned in to do my first line ever at twenty-eight years old and then . . . knock knock knock. The sound scared the shit out of me. My heart jumped in my chest. I wiped the cocaine off the dresser. Colin lost it. "What the fuck! That shit's expensive!" The knock was an invitation for a drink, which I declined. Colin stared at me, fuming. I had just knocked twenty dollars of coke on the ground. I was officially an idiot. Years into my addiction, I would ask Colin what I could get for twenty bucks. He replied, "Frustrated."

Colin was fuming, but he was determined to get me fucked up. This was his gift to me. He meant well. More coke was poured out onto my dresser. Again, my eyes saw myself leaning forward. The straw hovered above the little trail of evil for a second. Colin stood, smiling innocently. I inhaled deeply.

It felt great.

A rush of energy and calm all at the same time. My synapses fired. My eyes dilated. My breath was taken away. I didn't want more; I wanted to get back to the party. There wasn't any problem with this cocaine stuff. The media lied. This was my brain on drugs? Cool. A little sniffy sniff and back to my life. No big deal.

For the next twelve years, I wouldn't be able to remain sober for more than twenty days at a time.

Ironic. I provide assistance with daily living and housing. All my clients have a mental disability, but the vast majority have a history of substance abuse as well. Self-medication. Maybe that's why I identify with them so closely. Maybe we all have a mental health issue. More directly, we all decided to self-medicate. I would try to get sober, but nothing seemed to motivate me enough—not the birth of my two beautiful children, not Colin's cautionary tale, not the frustrated pleading from my loving wife. The call of addiction was strong, and I was so very weak.

I used to love to say that drugs sell themselves. Drug dealers don't advertise, yet we find them anyway. We ask and prod and survey the bar and figure out who is holding. Then we buy and buy and buy. We pester that motherfucker like we've known that joker for a hundred years. We call that prick at 4:00 a.m. and are incensed that he didn't answer the phone. "I thought you were a drug dealer, joker; get on your job!"

I have to take it all back. I erased the number of my dealer, so I don't recognize the sender of this text message I get one day. It reads: Got that good good on deck. I read it twice before I realize what the fuck it's talking about. Holy shit, this joker sent out a motherfucking bulletin. Now, that's a drug dealer. I'll put my dealer up against anybody's. That nigga is hustling. See, I've been around some sorry-ass dealers. Drug dealers who snort so much of their own shit they gotta cut the shit they sell with so much baby laxative you spend the rest of the night shitting and sniffing in your bathroom. Jokers who gotta go somewhere to get the shit. Go somewhere? Why the fuck you ain't bring that shit with you to the bar downtown we always hang out in and buy dope from you? Joker acts like he was surprised. "Oh, OK, you need some shit; I'll be right back." Yeah, I need some shit, motherfucker. We ain't friends; I don't want to know how your day was. I don't give a fuck if your girlfriend is on the rag and won't give you a blow job. *I want some coke!* Just like I did last week and the fifteen times you saw me before that.

But that text message was some new shit. I wasn't prepared for the new marketing plan. He came at me from left field. So I had to work to shrug it off. I text back: I'm not in town. He said OK. I know, I know. You're thinking, "You should have told him you quit." But see, that shit can never be said to your dealer. They laugh at that shit. That shit is the telltale sign of an oncoming relapse. If I had said that, he would've hit me with the "Oh OK, well, good luck with that." I don't need to hear that shit from him. This joker has sold me coke knowing I've been on a weeklong binge, eyes yellow from toxicity, and mouth white from dehydration. Good luck? He might as well say, "Yeah, right, asshole. See you tomorrow." So I did the right thing. Trust me; I know. But I saved his number just in case. Sobriety is the plan, a goal of mine, and that motherfucker said he had the "good good"; know what I'm saying?

Wouldn't it be wonderful to have one exact point where you know you hit rock bottom? Not like, oh, I don't know, ten. I should write a book called *The Vertex of Addiction*. But since I don't know the plural of vertex, it'll have to wait. I fucking hate those TV specials about stars hitting rock bottom and checking into some bullshit clinic to sober up. The junkie in me wants to believe that maybe Robert Downey, Jr. did clean up this time. If only Chris Farley's friends had seen it coming . . . Rick James died of exhaustion. In the end, you have choices; some lead you out of addiction. Some lead you deeper in. There is no rock bottom, just a soft mushy substance that, if you dedicate yourself and get really creative, you can surely dig deeper . . . much deeper.

I can't help it. I'm wired differently. Sensitive. Cocaine struck me. Took me. It rings me out and leaves me spent. But I keep coming back for more. Skipping work. Not eating. Hiding in plain sight. That's me watching TV. One of the guys on my school's football team turned out to be an LGBT rights activist later on. I remember turning on the television that day and seeing him on CNN or something, excessively manicured, tailored suit, and sporting a lisp. I was like, "Holy shit! I used to shower with that guy." I never would have picked him to be gay. I guess he would have never picked me to crawl around my apartment and lick coke dust from the carpet, but hey, here we are.

"Being an adult sucks," says every irresponsible adult. To those of us stuck in our past and unwilling to admit our role in the path chosen, adulthood does suck. But it started long before I considered myself an adult. It started in college. School had always been easy for me, but I had one teacher who hated me. It was mutual, of course. Cornelius was this short greasy-haired intense Catholic guy who spoke with a fake semi-British accent. I think he lived there for a summer when he was, like, twenty, and at sixty, he still felt it plausible to pretend he was an EastEnder. He always wore a green jacket like the one they give you for winning the Masters, but his had huge dandruff flakes embedded into the shoulder pads. He quoted obscure text in Latin and picked his nose obsessively. I'm not sure if he was gay or not. I mean, I never saw him fuck another guy in his ass or anything, but if it walks like a duck and quacks like a duck . . .

None of this bothered me, though. What rubbed me the wrong way was his insistence that I rewrite everything. Not just one or two papers, but all of them. He didn't give a shit if I composed pure *magnificus brainius* genius on a paper. He wanted a fucking rewrite. So I wrote and I wrote and then I wrote some more; it got to the point that I would have like four goddamn papers in various stages of development for this aloof son of a bitch. With Homecoming quickly approaching, something had to give.

I used to smoke American Spirit cigarettes at the time. OK, I still smoke American Spirits, but it must be noted that I was smoking at this particular time. So there—I said it. Anyway, I lit up one after the other and paced my penthouse apartment, which the Homecoming committee had so graciously provided. I had a rewrite due the next morning, but I couldn't for the life of me think of how anyone could expound on my thesis that the United States government should relax endangered species laws in poverty-stricken third-world countries. All night long, I pondered this question. I came up with nothing. The next morning, I decided to take a stand. I printed out the same damn paper I had handed in a week before. "Fucking prick probably won't even bother reading it." Like Martin Luther King, Malcolm X, and Mahatma Gandhi before me, I would not let the will of my oppressor deter me from my stated mission: the continuance of my pursuit of hot model pussy as president of the Homecoming committee.

I walked into Cornelius's classroom and flipped my paper on his desk. I noticed he didn't even glance at the goddamned thing. Class went as usual that day, so when he dismissed us, I dismissed him too. Mentally, I was already balls deep in that Afrocentric jawn who thought my aura was blessed. While waiting for my broadcast management class to start, I spied that dirty green jacket creeping toward me. "Master Earl." He had an irritating habit of calling everybody like we were in the royal court. Of course, coming from anyone else, it would have been received as common courtesy, but from him, it sounded condescending and downright uncomfortable. "Please follow me into my office." He closed the door and sat down, gripping my paper in his bony little hands. Damn, his nails were filthy.

Without even looking at me, he says, "Unacceptable." I'm thinking, *So what? I owe you a rewrite? Big fucking surprise.* Cornelius then looks me dead in the eye and says, "Apparently, you are unaware of the weight distribution of this paper in relation to this class." Cut to me looking completely confused. "If you are unable to execute the reproduction of this . . . paper . . . you will receive a failing grade in this class." Did that bastard just say I was going to fail? I know he didn't say I was going to fail. "You are dismissed, Master Earl."

Now panic began to set in. "Professor Cornelius, listen, I have a lot on my plate. Maybe you could reread the paper. It really isn't as bad as—"

"That will be all, Master Earl."

They say hindsight is twenty-twenty.

They usually say this after they curse out their professor in the professor's office: "You know what, John, yeah, you're not mister or professor. Just John, and you're a fucking asshole. Do you want to know why you're a fucking asshole? Well, I'll tell you why, John. That is probably the best goddamn paper you've ever read in your pitiful life, but it wouldn't matter to you, would it, John, because you like fucking with me. Well, fuck you, John! I don't need this class, I don't need this school, and I certainly don't need your condescending booger-picking approval." I probably added *faggot* in there somewhere, but I didn't want you to get the impression that I'm homophobic. What happened between then and rehab? Life. That was all my fault.

Rehab is tough. I've begun to see the world in a whole new light. Everything is an addiction. Sugar, coffee, television, salt, sex, exercise—the list goes on and on. Common denominator? All of the above make us feel really good. So of course I had to cut it all out. You got it, motherfuckers; I'm going cold turkey! That's right, and on top of that, I'm only eating organic shit. That expensive shit from Whole Foods where the cows don't do drugs, the bags are recycled, and the water is distilled. Hell, the goddamn drugs don't have drugs in them. Trust me, the pharmaceutical aisle is freaky in that joint. Everybody looks happy there, too, and I want to be happy. I like how they speak to one another and smile and help you out, and they don't leave their carts in the middle of the aisle like at the regular store that sells that garbage. I walked into the gas station the other day, and it took me two hours to find something to eat. Now that's progress. I'm going to be the healthiest man alive until the day I die.

I have an appointment with a personal trainer after work today. In my office, I'm half listening to this caseworker's idiotic requests for my new client. This is in part because I can't wait to get into the gym, but mainly because caseworkers are morons. They are always either condescending, stupid, or insane. This bitch is a triple threat. Whenever they begin to talk, my mind wanders off, and I just see their mouths moving, and I feel my head nodding, and I have no idea what they are saying. She is asking me to move my highest-paying client out of the room her client shares with her because her client is unhappy. The other evil incarnate in the room curses at her day and night. Calls her fat bitch and nasty bitch and the like. The caseworker is conveniently forgetting that her client is morbidly obese and shits the bed on a daily basis. I guess we've all got our issues, though. Caseworkers, please don't think that administrators care about the things you say or that you're eloquent or smart or anything. We just don't feel like being at work longer than we have to, so we nod and agree and apologize and hope you don't call the State. OK, good, we're done? I'm gone.

This trainer is trying to kill me. This is not a joke. Selwyn has muscles in his fingertips, and I can see why. But I am going to have a heart attack right here in the middle of Bally's Holiday Spa or Total Fitness or whatever the fuck they're calling it today. I've been here ten minutes, and he's got me doing an exercise that vaguely reminds me of pushups, but it involves a medicine ball and an extra movement that mimics asking the Lord for his forgiveness. This guy barely looked at my driver's license, let alone checked my vital signs, and my dumb ass already signed the waiver. Great. If I die, Bally's gets off scot-fucking-free, and I don't even have life insurance to soothe my wife's tears as she is interviewed on *The View*. Mental note: call New York Life before the next training session.

"One line is too many; a thousand is not enough." Steven's got my attention now. We haven't even been in a group for two minutes, and I know he's my savior. If I were casting the savior role in this movie, I would have picked the lead singer from the Pussycat Dolls, and then I would have had her become infatuated by my vulnerabilities and desperate cries for help. She would see me outside of the group and make passionate love to me in the shower by candlelight, but hey, I guess Steve will do. Shower scene not included.

I survey the room. These people don't have shit on me. I can sniff an eight-ball by myself in two days. One, if I don't have to go to work. That's an eight-ball motherfucker—an *eight fucking ball!* Almost four goddamn grams—I'm a motherfucking beast! What do these people do? Probably drink too much. That one lady probably pops schnapps in the kitchen in between loads of laundry. Big deal! I might need one on one with Steve because these people are bush-league addicts.

Wrong. Schnapps lady does have a drinking problem. The problem is she woke up two months ago in the drunk tank. Her car was totaled, and her five-year-old son was dead. She can't even remember getting behind the wheel. The snooty broad with the expensive jewelry also likes to drink. She's a high-level executive at some financial company. She has to entertain clients after work. In order to fit in, she throws a few back like one of the guys. She's been doing that three times a week since she started fifteen years ago. Now she finds she doesn't need the guys or clients in general in order to find a reason to throw a few back. Her marriage is on the rocks because apparently, she becomes quite the opposite of the ice lady we see sitting here when she's under the influence. I suppose hubby doesn't like to share. Of all the people in the group, only myself and Alex snort coke. Alex is married with two kids. Seems like a great guy. He's here because, after a night of snorting coke, he was too tired to go to the park with his wife and kids. He missed his second child's first steps and can't forgive himself. Shit, in my book that guy gets an A-plus. Missed the kid's steps and off to rehab? Wow! That guy has some character. He works for an insurance company, has his MBA and a great handicap. I'm sure he makes a ton of money, provides for his family, probably barbecues and shit, but he missed his kid's first steps, and he dives deep into depression. This is the kind of guy I need to hang out with. Maybe some of his characteristics will rub off on me. We'll go to the gym together, catch a movie. Grab some dinner and chill. Yeah, he'll be my new friend. I'll drop all those losers I hang out with. *I wonder if he's got a good connect?*

I dropped some coke in the bottom drawer of my file cabinet. My cook was walking in, and I didn't lock the door. It's really pissing me off. I mean, I know I'm supposed to be sober, but that little bit of coke won't hurt. These drawers are really tricky; they don't come out for some reason. They probably were built by sober people. Sober people have no idea what the fuck they're doing. I've considered clearing my desk and emptying the drawer of paperwork. Then turning the whole damn thing upside down on my desk. But that is just silly. Instead, I am in the process of building the world's longest straw. Sobriety be damned. I paid good money for that shit.

When I'm sniffing coke, I know I shouldn't be doing it. There is this little voice in my head that keeps saying, "OK, that's the last line. Put the straw down and go to sleep."

Then I tell that little voice, "It's already four a.m. I'm not going to sleep anyway, so I might as well finish this coke."

It says, "Do you want a heart attack?"

I say, "Well, maybe you'd shut the fuck up then."

Back and forth we go. Most of the time, I win, and so for the next couple of days, that little voice lets me have it. "Look at you—you're a fucking loser. Do you realize how much money you just spent? You'd be better off grabbing that 9mm and swallowing some shells." The depression gets pretty dangerous sometimes. That's when I see Marcus a lot. He doesn't say anything. I just see him. Lying there or suddenly rising up in bed. He always looks right at me. Unable to speak. Body ravaged by cancer. He doesn't judge me. Just disappointed.

I briefly imagine just driving off a bridge or something. I can envision the serenity of flying through the air. The quiet before I hit ground or water, the tranquility of death. Then I remember that I don't believe in the afterlife, and I grind my teeth, curse the heavens and my agnostic choices, and head toward the stinking office trying desperately to stay awake. I cannot concentrate on these days, so I pretend to be working on "proposals" at my computer. I feel utterly worthless. My life has reached a plateau. I am hemorrhaging cash due to my coke problems and bad investments. I just can't seem to get on track. You would think all that would be enough to make me quit. It is enough. Truly, it is. The problem is I get back on track. I start saving money. I start taking on more responsibility at work. Paying more attention to my wife. Volunteering. Networking. I start feeling good. I'm back on top. So surely I can handle a little sniff. Right?

My group counselor, Steve, is showing movies to the group today. I love when Steve shows movies because I don't have to share. Sharing is something you do when you're six and under. After that, it's every man for their goddamnselves as far as I'm concerned. I'm not the only one who feels this way. Our entire society is built upon selfishness. It's called capitalism. I am an affirmed capitalist. It is the one religion I agree with. See, it's fucked up if you're a Christian but still buy Nike sneakers manufactured by slave labor in communist China. Somewhere in your thinking, you have to believe that God has allowed those little girls with bleeding fingers to be exploited. I guess you say they will have their salvation when they reach his kingdom after sweating fifteen hours a day for five bucks a month for the next fifty years. That's a conflict.

Not for me, though. I'm a capitalist. All I think when I plunk down my $49.99 is "Nice fucking sneaks." Anyway, the point is we are watching movies today. It's all about how cocaine rewires your brain. Incredibly interesting material. Apparently, cocaine short-circuits the pleasure zones in the brain. It goes something like this:

The normal path to release dopamine in the brain is you run ten miles and feel good, bang, dopamine; or you go to dinner, chat for hours, bring the chick home, have sex and cum, bang, dopamine; or you study three years in law school, pass the bar, and get a high-paying job, bang, dopamine. Cocaine says, "Fuck all that shit." Take a sniff, bang, dopamine. Whoa, instant gratification. No muss, no fuss, with a money-back guarantee. Please note: nobody has ever asked for their money back. Because cocaine works. That's the big problem. You stop striving for real goals because you can have dopamine released when you want it, and everybody wants dopamine. It's what drives us to procreate, invent kitchen appliances, electric cars, space travel and get off welfare and climb mountains. Dopamine is why we are here. One particular part of the movie is especially disturbing. There is this experiment they talk about where somebody—in order to prove the addictiveness of cocaine—gave a mouse a bell, and every time the mouse rang the bell, they gave it some coke. Then they started making the mouse ring the bell more and more times in between coke shots. By the end of the experiment, the mouse rang the bell well over a thousand times for one shot of coke. They surmised that the mouse would probably kill itself ringing that bell for cocaine.

Bang. Dopamine.

My coke buddy Rick is an account executive. "Account executive" has a nice ring to it. Doesn't look bad on a business card either. Don't have to tell you how many strippers he's impressed. You already know. Rick no longer works there. Rick no longer does anything. He got locked up in front of a Wawa with coke stuffed all in his nose. I feel bad about that shit. I was supposed to be there with him. We should have both gotten caught. I stepped out to score a foot-long teriyaki chicken when the cops rolled up on him while he was shoving sugar booger into his cranium.

Rick is serving three years in a state penitentiary. I visited him once. I asked him how he was doing. What a stupid question. "I'm in prison, you rock head, how do you think I'm doing? I shower with men, genius, does that give you any clues? I jack off twice a day to the same picture of Aaliyah, and I know she's dead. Fuck you too."

Prison sucks. I've never spent a significant amount of time there, but it sure seems like it does. The food definitely sucks. You have to be tough too. Either be tough or join a gang. Rick changed his name to some Arabic shit I can't pronounce, but he's still using blow. He told me that Pablo has the best coke he's ever had. I find that strange. Don't they smuggle that shit in their assholes? Call me finicky, but anything that's been inside Pablo's ass is not going up my nose, at least not if I have concrete proof that it was, in fact, up Pablo's ass. The point is that Rick is still using. Me? I'm in rehab.

But I'm not sure which one of us is better off.

Hanging out in Northern Liberties, I met these advertising guys. They invited me to a party for a new client. A vineyard that was trying to capture the beer-drinking audience. So they wanted their wine associated with football and NASCAR and porn, and they were idiots because nobody is drinking wine when they watch NASCAR while betting football and jerking off. They were all Hollywood, and I hate Hollywood. It is the most insincere place on earth. In Hollywood, you cannot say *faggot*. You cannot say something is *gay*. I once spent an entire lunch with a friend of mine discussing how two big-time stars (whom I can't mention because they may figure out who she is and end her career) were gay, and she constantly kept looking around like the gay mafia was going to roll up and whack us. After a while, she had me looking over my fucking shoulder too. The thing is, everybody is gay out there. So what's the big fucking deal? Maybe I'm insensitive because I don't have any gay friends. Well, there is my buddy who has a penchant for ejaculating on chicks' tits and licking it off, but I'm not sure if that qualifies. Me? I just don't pull any punches, and I don't respect bullshit. Bullshit is a guy in Hollywood who makes his living being a sex symbol to women, paying starlets to date him, but takes a Bukkake shower from three guys in a hotel room on Sunset Boulevard. Dude, do you.

Anyway, I had been hanging in Northern Liberties for three months when Rick got out and came to visit. I hadn't even thought about cocaine in three, maybe four days. As soon as he touched down, he started pestering me to score. I had responsibilities to take care of. I didn't have time for that shit. I was trying to decide what toilet paper to switch the building to. So, of course, I blew off some steam with Rick. We went to this guy I knew in West Philly. His roommate sold coke. When Rick saw the size of the sack we got for $150, his eyeballs became the size of golf balls.

We partied all night long. We went from club to club, always taking time to hand off the bag and dip in the bathroom. Unable to lay lines across a table, Rick showed me a special technique of getting a bump out of a baggie. You pinch what you want to the top, stick your straw in, and sniff. I have to admit, it was one of the best times I've ever had. By the time we reached the third club, I was drunk off my rocker. Another side effect of cocaine is that it builds your "tolerance" up, allowing you to ingest way more alcohol than you previously thought possible. Needless to say, my bladder was screaming for relief once again, and I grabbed our bag of happiness and stumbled my way to the bathroom.

Oh thank God, I thought as I entered the single-stall bathroom. Club owners who build single-stall bathrooms truly understand the needs of the drug-addicted and sexually promiscuous patrons who keep them in business. I closed the door and relieved myself. The next move was to get a bump from our bag. I don't know how I did it or, more specifically, how I did it without fucking dying, but I sniffed the whole bag. *The whole fucking bag!* Man, was Rick pissed. He couldn't believe it. The rest of the night, he just kept looking at me. To this day, he probably thinks I did that shit on purpose. I couldn't get my friend on the phone after that, so we were out of coke for the night. It showed me two things. First thing was that cocaine was something people would definitely fight over. Rick's face had rumble written all over it. The second thing was that I had one hell of a tolerance level for cocaine.

Let the binges begin.

Today is the Fourth of July. Julia down the street is having a barbecue on the rooftop of her building. I'm rolling with my new buddy, City Councilman Luke. This could really solidify my position in the city. Life isn't about your grades or your degree or your expertise. It's about who you know and what they think about you. Rick taught me that. I read one of Rick's presentations. I don't think his marketing ideas could have sold Christians on salvation, but he knew every bartender in town and fucked all his female clients. Therefore, they stayed with his company. He was good for the bottom line. His coworkers, on the other hand, would spend weeks preparing masterfully designed and expertly produced proposals, only to have clients stare blankly at them after the presentation. Not me. I need this fucking contract with the city. They pay triple the amount SSI does. Triple. Shiiiiit. This guy is going to get the Rick treatment.

Luke was a new councilman, and I had thrown a little shitty fundraiser for him. I only raised $3K for him, but to a councilman, that was huge. These people would give you a blow job for five bucks. His sister, Colleen, was all over me. They were some Irish Catholic Roxboro white kids. I'm not racist or anything; I'm just stating the facts. If she had been black, I would have said she was black, but she was Irish. The reason I mention this is that she was pale. Extremely pale. Vampire pale. I guess the hipsters and weed and alcohol and mushrooms made her feel free.

So up there on the rooftop, we started drinking. We started with Johnny Walker Black, then we moved to shots of Patron. By the time we started throwing back drinks, Colleen was grabbing my jeans and whispering in my ear. She wanted me, her bed, and a bag of coke. Ding, ding, ding! The magic words had been spoken. I hailed us a cab, and we were at her spot in a flash. Her place was . . . interesting. Fuck that, her room was scary. She had German scat porn and bondage materials and whips and chains. The bed had little bags scattered in it and obviously had not been changed since she got into town. Stains from her previous night's activities were evident. She sat on the edge of the bed sniffing coke on her night table discussing what seemed to me an unusual obsession with Madonna. We had sex. Wish I could tell you something about it. Too much coke had turned me numb. I kind of watched us fucking like animals. She bit my ear and asked me to "shit on her." She went for some towels in the bathroom. This was too much for me; I grabbed my clothes and jumped out the window. I literally got dressed in an alley and ran down the street. I have never been a part of such a disturbing scene in my entire life. I took the hottest, longest shower of my life when I got home. I didn't get that city contract.

Gotta work on my sales technique. That's cocaine.

12

MONEY MONEY MONEY…MONEY

I hate when wealthy people give their money to the destitute. The destitute can't really appreciate that money. If Angelina Jolie gives $1.3 million to the country of Cambodia over five years, what does that do? Well, it looks great in the headlines. We all applaud her. We have a dinner in her honor. I'm not saying her heart isn't in the right place or that she's doing it for the publicity; just maybe those funds would be better utilized by a married father of two making $80,000 per year. That guy sits up every night in his bed wondering how to start his own business, will they raise his adjustable-rate mortgage, and how the hell is he going to pay for private school? If he got some money from her, it would not only change his life; he would be able to change others' lives. It's almost like they don't want him to get ahead. Maybe because they don't want you to get ahead.

Those living in abject poverty should get in line behind him. It's like that old Reagan-era trickle-down theory. When I win the lottery, I'll say, "Fuck the poor" and start a nonprofit organization aimed at the upwardly mobile. All the suburbs will be a buzz with this new Svengali of the middle class. I'll be like Tony Robbins, only I'll include giving away cash so you can actually do all the things I'm talking about at my conventions. Not just buy my fucking tapes and get pumped up before you clock in at your day job. Then I'll require that everybody give me a minority share of their company in return for the loot I gave them. The middle class will be able to afford private school and McMansions. The poor will be employed by the middle class and be able to afford food and stuff. And Angelina Jolie will kiss my ass. Kiss my black ass, Angelina!

That's all bullshit.

My mother and father were both born into abject poverty. They pulled themselves up from nothing and created the city's largest private-owned residential care network. They worked their asses off and passed none of their work ethic on to me. I'm spoiled. I'm a brat. It's almost unavoidable for people in my position. It's a precarious state to be in, and it's not to be envied. With success and money come neglect, miscommunication, heartache, and pain. Although I don't get along with them, I do respect them, and it's hard to respect some of the client families I encounter.

What right do I have to be disgusted by them? What right do I have to sit in judgment of these poor souls? I built nothing. Earned nothing. The only thing I did right was being born into the right family. I swam faster than the other sperm. I won the gene-pool lottery, and I have the nerve to look over my desk at this woman and look down on this woman and judge this woman.

Rita is so fucking fat. Why are so many poor people fat? You would think that with limited funds, food would be hard to come by. Apparently not. Welfare feeds them. No, welfare anchors them. By providing unfettered access to junk food and no requirements on health care, welfare hooks them. They develop an addiction to the free food and the free money, and they cannot break the cycle. They mature through generations of poverty. If you give a man a fish, he will eat for a day, but if you teach a man to fish he will eat for a lifetime. Which would you do if you were selling fish? Welfare doesn't teach. Welfare has no intention of teaching. The livelihoods of millions of government workers, politicians, and corporations depend on a certain percentage of our population remaining ignorant, obese, and unemployed. Can't you see, Rita? They are using you. You are a pawn. Nothing is for free.

She has come to check her brother into Argyle Street. The two of them sit in my office: fat, stupid, and poor. I am their savior. You can see the years of poverty carved into their faces. It's lack of proper nutrition. Lack of proper health care. It's just *lack*. Embodied. Rita oozes into the chair. It's obvious by the smile on her face that her brother is a real fucking problem. In my business, the worse the client is, the happier the family/social worker/hospital is to place them with me. Their lack of funds seems to intensify this feeling.

Rita and Ricky Sparks. Twins. Their mother died two years ago and left them nothing but a dilapidated house in North Philly and each other. Rita was the higher functioning of the twins and had taken over the family affairs. Ricky was placed in the basement where he proceeded to descend into a madness they hadn't experienced previously. He hadn't bathed for months, and he was eating raw chicken that he was washing in the toilet. The family didn't investigate anything until the stench of feces had permeated the home so badly that the neighbors called the health department. The toilet had been clogged with raw chicken parts, yet that hadn't stopped old Ricky from continuing to defecate and clean chicken in the toilet.

Why hadn't he used the tub?

Rita sat and tried to convince me that not only was Ricky "not a big problem," but that he was actually highly intelligent. Yeah, sure, Rita. Unbathed, shit-chicken-eating Ricky seems like a real fucking Mensa member. And that's when Ricky started to speak. Oh my, Ricky could speak. He droned on and on about nothing about everything. His mouth was spastic and caked with thick saliva. The breath hit me and offended my nostrils in a manner I hadn't thought possible. He was revolting. He was condescending. And he was fucking funny. All at the same time. Holy shit, he was hilarious. Damon Wayans used to play a character named Oswald Bates on *In Living Color* who would make up and misuse multisyllabic words in an attempt to sound intelligent:

> First of all, we must internalize the "flatulation" of the matter by transmitting the effervescence of the "Indianisian" proximity in order to further segregate the crux of my venereal infection. Now, if I may retain my liquids here for one moment. I'd like to continue the "redundance" of my quote, unquote "intestinal tract," you see, because to preclude on the issue of world domination would only circumvent—excuse me, *circumcise* the revelation that reflects the "Afro-disiatic" symptoms which now perpetrates the Jheri curls' activation. Allow me to expose my colon once again. The ramification inflicted on the incision placed within the Fallopian cavities serves to be holistic, taken from the Latin word *jalapeno*

And his twin idiot, Rita, just as pleased as Mama at the church piano recital, just smiling all the while. Where the fuck am I?

Ricky was broke, of course. He received only two

hundred bucks per month, which Rita claimed she had to pay for his storage unit. Why? What is it about stuff that people love? I detest stuff. I can't think with clutter around me. The thought of paying for a room full of shit that is even more useless to me than the rooms full of shit in my own home is fucking obscene to me. For some reason, they thought the babbling poster boy for voluntary salmonella poisoning would one day care for his own apartment, so they just had to save all his shit. I mean, God forbid they just go to Ikea, right?

So Ricky moves in. We put him on the third floor in a tiny room with Joseph D., a "brittle diabetic" and chronic bitcher and moaner who insists on visiting his physically disabled girlfriend once a month, twenty miles away by cab. Joe has uncontrollable dandruff, and Ricky is filthy. They are a match made in heaven. Heart emoji.

Their room is a 120-square-foot haven for squalor. The staff try their best to clean but are hindered by Ricky's fondness for his bed. Incidentally, we have found that Ricky is light skinned. Let me back up. When Ricky first came in, he had splotches all over him. He looked like a Down syndrome leopard. I assumed he had some sort of aggressive strain of vitiligo. The truth is more disturbing. His lack of hygiene attention had led to dirt embedding into his pores, and over time, the pores clogged, creating large, round dark spots all over his body. I walked into work one day and didn't recognize Ricky. He was . . . light. Really light.

I wonder how long he had gone without bathing. He was talking, but I couldn't concentrate. I just kept staring and wondering how long I could go. I mean, sure, sometimes after the gym and work all day, I might pass out without a shower, and I admit that's disgusting. I have even left the house after some morning sex with a dirty dick, but damn, my shit never turned colors. Then *ahh!* Ricky leaned in to get my attention. His breath. His awful breath. My eyes were stinging. My stomach convulsed. Those actors on dopey sitcoms who I thought were overly dramatic when they mimic someone holding back vomit had my respect. It was fucking awful. It was reprehensible. The stench filled my nose and invaded me. It grabbed my soul and shook it violently, slapped it around, abused it sexually, and discarded it, stench covered, on my desk. I felt like I was going to black out. I had to stand and try to get some air. I was drowning in the reek end of foul. When was the last time he brushed his fucking teeth? Where was the window? Had he been eating shit? What the fuck am I doing here? I have a goddamn degree!

Like I said, his improvement was tremendous under our care. And so, of course, his sister refused to pay. Well, she paid, but she wouldn't pay the full amount. I applied and applied for state supplement funds, but nothing ever came through . . . according to his sister. I was forced to use evasive maneuvers. I called Social Security and impersonated Ricky, which wasn't that hard, seeing as nobody knew him at Social Security. The government paper pusher answered the line, sounding as if she was half-comatose from apathy and ready to hang up on me if I uttered the slightest incorrectness. I knew my shit and jumped through all her hoops. She put me on hold and I waited. And waited . . . and waited. Ricky's state supplement had been approved months prior. His check had been deposited directly into the joint account his sister controlled: $6,789.45, to be exact.

You don't necessarily open a residential care facility to get rich. You open it because your heart yearns to care for the forgotten souls wandering the earth. You want to help them in some small way. In return, however, it is expected that you will receive some sort of consideration. The state of Pennsylvania deems thirty-four dollars per day sufficient. I would wholly disagree, but that is neither here nor there. To have that measly sum ripped from your grasp after you sweat and toil to drag that discarded wretch up from the trash heap of human existence is heartbreaking. Rita moved Ricky home soon thereafter. I didn't call Social Security and report her. I didn't call a lawyer to pursue her for the funds.

I recalled years earlier we had a twenty-six-year-old Asian guy in the building. He refused to eat breakfast. Not important to the story, but true. Turns out he didn't speak English and couldn't communicate to us that he hated eggs. If he had stayed, I would have received a violation for not hiring an interpreter. Anyway, we applied for a supplement for him, and it came through. Back then we got paper checks that needed to be endorsed by the client. I climbed the stairs to the guy's room and opened the check. He may not have spoken English, but he damn sure could read it. Eight thousand six hundred bucks and his name on it. In my mind, he karate chopped me, swiped the check, jumped out the second-floor window, tumble-rolled the front yard, and sprinted down the street. Racist, I know, but fuck him. He took the check, stuffed it in his underwear, and walked out, leaving all his earthly possessions . . . and me high and dry.

Yeah, you're welcome.

13

YES, MA'AM

I don't watch the local news, mostly because it's nothing but bullshit entertainment masquerading as information. Why is Susie Han, hot Asian reporter, always sent out to the scene of the crime eight hours after the crime occurred to stand in an empty field so that she can point to a random street where *xyz* happened blah, blah, blah? Are we that desperate for details? Who the fuck cares? Just tell me what happened. A random tree shot doesn't do shit for me. Also, the amount of reporting of bad shit is epidemic. Our country is actually safer than it's ever been. Unfortunately, "Black Man Drops His Daughter at Preschool Before Opening His Insurance Office Every Day" doesn't quite grab anybody's attention. Hell, I'm not sure anybody is gonna wanna read this shit.

Winter is a strange time for my building. The world

becomes cold; the trees are barren, and the ardently homeless have to decide whether to risk frostbite and death or succumb to the inherent risks of shelters—or worse . . . the rules of a personal care boarding home. It isn't until that time of year that we truly realize how alone these people are. We are their everything. Their mother/father/sister/brother all rolled into one. Ninety percent of residents don't have any family members visit during the year or take them home, and that number remains constant throughout the holiday season.

My earliest memories are of this time of year. Not like you might expect. I don't remember drinking eggnog and opening gifts while Dad smoked his pipe in his favorite easy chair, smiling knowingly while I tried to stay up hoping to glimpse Santa Claus. No, I remember the green chairs in the living room on Durham Street adorned with the decayed minds of discarded humans and the basement where I played while Mom prepared Thanksgiving/Christmas/New Year's feasts. The meals all ran together. The holidays did the same. Then, I stayed in the basement, hoping she wouldn't call me to eat upstairs, praying we could go home. That basement was my sanctuary, the one tangible reminder that my parents had thought of me. They had placed a ping-pong table and—well, that's about it, but at least the goddamned residents weren't allowed down there. I was growing to hate them, almost as much as my parents. Parenting doesn't come with an instruction manual, and all children end up blaming their parents for their shortcomings on some couch eventually. But I felt a particular seething indignation at my family for forcing me to spend the holidays with these people.

We were here every day. After school. Before school. Days off, and weekends. Every. Single. Day. The life of a looney bin child: it never stopped. The business engulfed our lives like so many planktons by a whale. I tried hard to swim away, but attempts at escape were futile. Why, just once, couldn't we spend that time of year alone? Hire someone to watch the crazies and sit at home in our pajamas and eat pumpkin pie and drink eggnog and watch the lights flicker on the tree?

I stared at my mother as she loaded the car full of gifts for the residents. I was begging her to stay home, to leave me home. Not out loud, but with my eyes just staring at her. No tears back then. I never cried back then. Maybe that's why I'm so prone to doing it now. I never showed emotion back then. Stone-faced. It was encouraged. "Don't be so thin skinned," my mom would say in her Jamaican accent (never pronouncing her *h*'s). That's me pleading through the window, "'Elp me."

I was hurried into the station wagon and off to the home we went . . . again. I decided that day she was no longer my mom. I wouldn't call her mom; I would call her ma'am. I showed her no affection. Didn't hug her or kiss her or refer to her as anything other than ma'am for one year. Well, maybe it was less than a year, but my determination was strong and my memory weak.

We spent every holiday there as usual. We decorated the boarding home for each holiday with the sad paper turkeys and pilgrims dangling around the dining room, the stick-figure tree for Christmas, and the streamers and top hats for New Year's Eve.

That's why I didn't want to follow in their footsteps. I didn't want my children to feel the neglect and jealousy that I felt. I didn't want them to feel like anything was more important than them ... I didn't want them to call me "sir."

I failed at finding alternative sources of income, but I never spent a holiday at my facility. Until I did. Thanksgiving 2012 was going to be just like all the rest. I was wrapping up my day early (well, earlier than usual) since I was never a fan of working overtime when I was the boss. A commotion in the hallway dragged me out of my routine. Before I reached the hallway, a barrage of "motherfuckers" and "goddamn niggers" combined with the crashing of porcelain created a petrifying discord.

I stepped into the hallway in time to dodge his pants. I stepped back into the hallway in time to see his soiled adult diaper ripped from his groin and hurled into the TV room. I heard them gasp at the offensive contents and knew I had to move quickly. There are many things they teach you in administrator courses about what paperwork is needed for this, that, and the third, yet they teach you virtually nothing about people. They can't. How could someone describe this scene in a textbook or workshop? Who was going to play diaper man in the training seminar at 8:30 a.m.? In order to deal with the mentally unstable, you have to remain flexible; you have to be patient. Most importantly, no matter what you are faced with—whether it's a knife-wielding white boy named Abdul sprinting at you in the middle of the street or this elderly man performing a repulsive diaper striptease—you have to appear to be completely unfazed and in control. I walked out into the corridor. My staff was keeping their distance from Henry. Henry was old—like, really fucking old. His hair was gray and patchy, and he was skinny. He was foaming at the mouth and screaming obscenities. His eyes were wide with crazy. The staff was scared as shit. So was I.

I looked Henry dead in his crazy fucking eyes as I walked swiftly up to him. This was some *Wild Kingdom* shit, and I had to establish who was the alpha male. He squinted at me as I approached. He crouched down low. I wasn't sure if he was going to attack me, but I kept advancing and barking instructions. It reminded me of the scene in *Full Metal Jacket* when the sergeant walks in on Pyle in the bathroom. Glad Henry didn't have an AK. He turned and sprinted. Never seen a human run that fast. Well, white boy Abdul was kind of quick when he took off down the street, but I did gun my engine at his crazy ass. He had a knife, y'all. Anyway, Henry was bound for upstairs, and I let out a barely visible sigh of relief.

Too soon. Before I could walk up the stairs, I heard more porcelain crashing and more blasphemous cursing, and this time, he was addressing me by name. "Fuck you, Earl, you goddamn pussy faggot nigger." Hmm, that's not how to address the alpha male. I reached the top step and faced him in the hallway. My staff kept three steps behind me.

I have only been in a few fights in my life, but I know the cardinal rule is that he who strikes second loses . . . or something like that. I felt myself sprinting toward him. As I tackled the naked skinny old man, I swear I saw a half smile. I took him down, but he was strong. My mother always said don't fight with crazy people; they get a strength from the other side. Well, she wasn't fucking lying. Henry may have been seventy-eight and skeletal, but fuck, he was strong. He twisted and turned, and we fought and wrestled for dominance. I tried to act calmly, but this motherfucker was winning. Finally, I got him face down and jammed my knee into his back. The staff was instructed to call 911, and that is where I held him until Philly's finest showed up.

The officers seemed incredulous at a young man subduing an elderly gentleman in that manner, until I released my hold. Henry promptly sprung to his feet and charged the squad. He was incapacitated within seconds and hauled away to the CRC. The CRC is where we "302" you, at least that's what we call it here in Philly. Involuntary commitment in the crisis response center. I can send almost anybody there for twenty-four hours. Scary, right? Henry needed to go. So, he went.

Next order of business was paperwork. My favorite. It was Thanksgiving Day, and I was about to file a fucking incident report. Never mind that my building was in shambles, there was a shitty diaper smeared throughout the TV room, the residents had witnessed an assault of sorts, and I had torn a button off my custom shirt from Ventresca's because the state wanted its fucking paperwork. If an inspector had walked in right then and there, he wouldn't have cared if I consoled the clients or staff or any of that trivial bullshit. He'd make sure I knew I had twenty-four hours to file a report. He would want to see Henry's file to determine whether I placed notations indicating that he might strip his diaper off and break all my lamps. He would check my old violations to see if there were any repeats due to the latest incident. He would then sit for an hour in my office—far, far away from the clients he supposedly protects, far away from the vulnerable people that he swore to advocate for—and he would write his report. His report would undoubtedly end up in a fine for me for some bullshit: 85A or 108C or something. Something to give me a fine, something to give me a warning, something to let me know they were the boss and that no matter whatever happened in these homes, no matter how ridiculous or strange or completely out of the realm of normal existence, I was to blame. Me. And then they would leave.

So while interviewing the staff instead of frying my turkey, I discovered a funny thing. Henry had been fine all week. Hell, Henry was always fine. He had dementia and Alzheimer's disease sprinkled with a little splash of schizophrenia. He barely knew what galaxy he was in. Fine, until his daughter called Thanksgiving Day. She didn't call to say she loved him; she called to inform him she wasn't going to have him over for dinner. Well, was he expecting her to? No. Was she breaking a long-standing tradition? No. She just wanted to call her father, whom she rarely saw after she dropped him off two years ago, to say, "Hey, you know, you are not being picked up for the holidays, right?" Aww. Now, that's Daddy's little girl. Well, ol' Henry promptly flew into a rage. The phone call reminded him of where he was and what was going on and maybe more importantly what was not going on. Shit, I'm sure he didn't even know it was Thanksgiving before she fucking called. The human side of me wanted to call the little bitch and tell her what a miserable fucking cunt she was and how I hoped her husband tripped on a dirty sock while she was sucking his dick, and he suffocated her before breaking her neck. Instead, I filed my report with the state (without mention of my remedy of death by fellatio).

You know the State came out. You know they investigated. You know what they found. As usual, yours truly had been neglectful. I had the nerve not to have put measures into place to ensure that residents were mentally prepared (that means distracted) for the holiday season. Their recommendation was for me to increase my activity calendar and to place these egregious crimes on my violation report on the internet for everyone to see. I always wondered why the State never placed my good deeds on the website. Aren't the State and I on the same side? Shouldn't we be? Doesn't my work reflect their training and regulation? Wouldn't it be nice and smarter marketing if they mentioned the other thirty-eight people who had an oven-fresh turkey dinner with mashed potatoes, macaroni and cheese, cranberry sauce, greens, stuffing,

and . . .

and . . .

and . . .

Nobody cares, right? Good news is no news at all.

All those years I spent at the homes, wishing we were like "normal" families. Wishing we were driving somewhere to visit family. I get it now. I wasn't spending Thanksgiving and Christmas away from my family; they were.

"Earl, can you go wake Mrs. Jackson for dinner?"

"Yes, ma'am."

14

LOCATION, LOCATION, LOCATION

So I'm sitting in the waiting room of Einstein Hospital's psych ward. I know they only call me for their "hard to place" clients. They only call me when they can't get rid of someone. They call me for the ex-felon/rapist/meth addict with no source of income. Social workers have no souls. They dump people on the streets as soon as their insurance stops paying for the bed. Well, I suppose it's more the insurance companies who won't pay and the hospital administrators who demand the beds be released, and then the social worker has to make tough decisions, and those decisions sometimes involve calling up providers and lying through their fucking teeth. Hey, just doing their jobs. The economics of health care don't trickle down to the mentally disabled, at least not in Pennsylvania.

They told me she was young and bipolar, yet pleasant,

and needed a place to stay. Schizophrenics can be admitted over the phone. They are a dime a dozen, but bipolar is a different animal altogether. You truly don't know what you are getting. One minute, they're sweet like a puppy on Christmas wearing a fluffy sweater, and the next minute, they'll put the puppy in a blender and hit puree.

Problem for me is that I am always too desperate for income. The government only gives us thirty-four dollars a day to ensure I stay that way, so here I am about to interview Stacy. People don't become crazy at age forty or fifty; they start out as crazy. Some reveal their craziness earlier than others. You never know when that switch will flip.

Stacy had been kicked out of her family home for the fourth time and hospitalized here at Einstein. Her parents just couldn't deal with her anymore. Stacy had been this way since birth. The whole family had been living inside a hurricane—Hurricane Stacy—and they were fed up. Her chart was thick. Her chart was scary. She tried to drown a neighbor's child once. Several small animals were found dead in their family shed. Law enforcement had a long relationship with her, dating back to thirteen years old when she stole her teacher's car and drove to New Jersey to buy liquor and stay three days in a motel with her very first pimp. Aww, what a cutie, right?

She had a younger sister who was "normal," and they were trying to help her navigate through her senior year of high school. Stacy's random bipolar episodes were threatening to destroy their lives. She was a cutter and a prostitute and a liar and young and I was desperate to fill a bed.

The social worker's forehead dripping with sweat threatened to reveal either how bat-shit crazy Stacy was or how serious her drug addiction was, but who was I to judge? Shit, I was high too. Stacy was working too hard to maintain control of the interview. Ms. Social Worker Lady sat us in a completely white room with a garage-sale bookshelf filled with dusty tomes. The books were supposed to convince outsiders that something besides warehousing was going on here, that these wretched souls were receiving beneficial activities and social time during their stay. The truth of the matter was these people were numbers: digits in an accountant's ledger. Notches on a belt. Dollar signs.

Stacy was very young. Extremely young. Twenty-four years young. Never-seen-rabbit-ears-on-a-goddamned-television young, and *she* was interviewing *me*. Umm, what? It was comical, and I watched myself from afar. This young crazy white female interviewing this older (seasoned?) bearded black man. I could see her mouth moving and my head nodding and the caseworker laughing. I must be saying something funny. My mind wandered as it tends to do. My antennae saw no reason to raise at her nervous laugh and plastered smile. She was overmedicated—a telltale sign that she was extremely dangerous. She decided she wanted to live under the supervision of this bearded black stranger, and since I was too embarrassed to admit I had been staring out the window, I admitted her into the home. Eh, fuck it.

Stacy was . . . needy. She commanded way too much of our time and energy from the moment she walked through the door. I completely understand her parents now. She was depressed and lonely and a failure and couldn't get things started and felt her life was over.

and . . .

and . . .

and . . .

She was just like me.

That's me in that chair, realizing I'm crazy too. Not just quirky and weird and funny, but maybe actually crazy. She sounds like *me*. I sound like *her*.

Stacy is in my office crying uncontrollably about the life she has squandered and the impossibility of correcting her wrongs. She desperately wants to move forward but cannot for the life of her decide which direction that is in. I feel like I am listening to a female voice in my own head. Is this what I am? A heaving mess of sobbing insanity? What do other people think of me for real? Stacy is avoided at all costs by the staff and, increasingly, the residents as well. Am I the plague of my crew? Maybe that's why everyone moved to California. Maybe that's why I wasn't invited on the Punta Cana birthday trip. Maybe that's why they don't include me in their money deals. Maybe I'm really fucking paranoid. Which means I'm crazy. God, this is unnerving. Now I'm sweating, and I can't breathe. Am I talking to myself? The panic attacks are coming back. I can't ride that wave. Not in front of Stacy, my sister in crazy. Not in front of anyone. Surf's up.

When I first got into the family business, I envisioned myself sitting behind a great big desk while making important business decisions. I would dress in tailored suits and fine shoes while I grew the business into a national corporation. It never got there. I never was able to maneuver my way to that point—whether it was my mother's vehement reluctance to relinquish control or my wanton spending habits and addictions. I woke up twenty years later and was in the same spot I started out in. It was depressing and lonely and scary, and Stacy was like a fucking mirror sitting across my desk.

It doesn't make sense to compare yourself to others. It doesn't make sense to link Stacy and me, but my brain couldn't help it. I had a six-figure income, traveled the world, sent my kids to private school, and allowed my wife to explore an artistic (but not lucrative) path, yet I felt like I was the same as Stacy. Stacy, the bipolar escort who cut herself and rammed her head into the walls of her family home while her sister tried desperately to study her way out of the madhouse. Were we all that different? She wanted more, and she didn't know how to get it. She was frustrated and felt trapped. I, too, felt the suffocation of the world.

· · ·

Jessie interrupted our session. I thought I would get a respite. She couldn't be as bad as Stacy. Couldn't be. I was becoming a bit frayed at the edges with Stacy. Stacy stared at me with big pleading eyes, yet I just didn't have any more emotional bandwidth for her. I was running low. On fumes. Please, Stacy, just go upstairs and get lunch or a nap or a shower. Please.

Jessie was no walk in the park, mind you. She plopped down in the chair across from me. Her white hair, cut into low bangs, barely hid her frantic eyes dancing around my office. She bit her fingernails and adjusted thrift-store clothing incessantly. She smelled like forgotten days. She, too, felt the weight of the world. Jessie had previously worked at a large pharmaceutical company when she had a mental breakdown. She walked into her office completely naked, screaming and crying. She didn't believe she had enough money to put on clothes but didn't want to lose her job, so she came to work anyway. Dedication. She was deathly afraid of not having enough money to live. Enough to eat. She was still afraid. She was right to be.

How many of us live these secret crazy lives? Opening our doors and feigning normalcy, we walk our children to the bus stop and kiss them goodbye as we head for the downtown train—drowning our misery in the Katy Perry pouring through our earbuds. How many psychopaths are pretending to read the *Wall Street Journal*, while deep inside the envy they feel for their neighbors' house or clothes or lifestyle is bubbling into a murderous rage? Then right when it reaches the tipping point, the train slides up to their destination, and they snap into reality, exit the train, and hop onto their hamster wheel. We try hard to hold on to what we think we should—our material possessions and our connections and our accomplishments—but it never seems enough. Never seems enough! Through it all, we smile and exchange pleasantries and reduce our carbs and wear our Fitbits. And die ... slowly.

These breaks with the norm are jarring, not just because of their social inappropriateness but because they are mirrors.

How many people at the bus stop would love to slap their neighbor and tell them to shut that fucking dog up or kiss them deeply, inappropriately full on the mouth or tell them how much they hate the little figurines that they have placed ever so carefully around their abode? How many people are hiding an addiction or poverty or abuse or any of a number of things? We are all crazy in some way, and these outbursts are disturbing because they hit home. They show you how close you are to losing it.

Hiding is sanity.

Jessie found herself living in personal care homes, paranoid, divorced, and obsessed with money. Or rather, the perceived lack thereof. Although she had $35,000 in total savings and a monthly income of $1,700, she still felt broke. Never mind that the average resident in these homes had zero in savings and a monthly income of $655; it was her perception that shaped her reality. Perception. All of us shape our own reality. In her reality, everyone was doing better than her. She couldn't stand the drive to the program because the happiness of the people walking to and from wherever they were going reminded her of what she had lost and how she would never get it back again. Another fucking mirror.

Isn't that all of us, though? Staring at Facebook and Instagram and Snapchat and whatnot, wishing we were on vacation or grinding or at the concert or playing in the game or just doing something different than what we are doing? Wishing we were somewhere else or, better yet, someone else? And what about those people tantalizing us on their pages with their exotic lifestyles? Telling us how wonderful their lives are. Teasing us with their cars and shoes and bags and boats and asses and abs. Who do they wish they were?

Jessie rambles on at a voracious clip. She bites her nails and violently fidgets while explaining how she is going to end up naked and broke and dead without ever finishing her paperwork. Her van is late today. Her meds are wearing off today. I am wearing thin today. She receives electroshock treatment, which makes her forget all her worries. Today . . . not like the old days with the woodblock in your mouth and fifty thousand watts zapped through your skull using electrodes. Now, they give you a little pill. One little pill short-circuits your brain. Zap. Zombie. You come back home, and you can't remember where you've been or why you went. She barely remembers her name and certainly can't remember mine. She knows she used to be worried about money but can't remember why. She needs to get to the program.

Stacy slinks away out of sight, and Craig's skeletal frame stands in the doorway watching over his new girlfriend Jessie. I look at the scene. This is my life. I wish Earl and Jackie had opened a restaurant. There are a lot of flies circling Craig. He probably hasn't washed in days, even though he spends hours on end in the bathroom. You would think he could take a shower during his coke binges. You're right there, Craig. Right fuckin' there. Jessie is whining about something. I am thinking about Craig's coke addiction, or is it mine?

And then all hell breaks loose.

The alarm in our building isn't mechanical; it's human. The sound it makes is my name. It's calling me now. It's shrill. I have to spring to action like this all means something to me. Like I care. Stacy has been here for one week. One fucking week. She is the neediest person I have ever come into contact with in this business. She whines, she cries, she frets, she demands. She fucking sucks. She has taken it to another level now, though.

The staff is gathered around her door as I sprint up the stairs. The Jamaican accents fire information at me, and I wish I had a good reggae beat. The door is barricaded shut. Stacy is screaming and crying from the other side that she is going to kill herself. Well, kill yourself already, Stacey! You have been nothing but a fucking pain in the ass (and a mirror to my face) since you got here. You don't like the food, and the shower is cold, and the heat doesn't work, and the residents are too old (I told you the fucking residents were too old!), and John is creepy, and there are too many stairs, and the neighborhood is dangerous, and you call my wife's cell phone every night, and you demand meetings with me every day. I mean, fuck, bitch, kill yourself. (I didn't really say that . . . out loud).

We had already removed all razor blades from the floor and didn't allow her to eat with knives. What the fuck does she have in there? A ballpoint pen? The police are already on their way, and we are trying to talk her out of this decision. Can you imagine the paperwork for this? Fucking nightmare. The entire building can hear Stacy whining in her room, lamenting the lack of success in her life. She is screaming out for help. For attention. Finally, the cavalry comes.

Ironic how settling the sight of blue uniforms can be at times. Unless you are a black male being stopped in a white neighborhood after dark, of course; then shit is very fucking unsettling, but I digress. I now no longer had to be in charge or responsible, and my stress levels dropped. In the middle of chaos, I was calm. Not pretending to be calm, but really calm. I felt blissful. Is this all I wanted? Just to be one of the crowd? Not the man in charge or *el presidente* or the decider? Just a witness, able to view the carnage and return home. The cops seemed to relish their roles as well.

They asked her nicely . . . once. The door exploded inward, and as it shattered, the bed barricade was transported across the carpet in Stacy's bedroom. (That's going to be expensive.) I couldn't see Stacy, but I could imagine her fear. The officers seemed so confident and matter-of-fact. They waltzed into her room like they had been there a thousand times before. She was crouched under the window, sobbing and muttering as spit mixed with tears. The officers were almost by her side, reaching out passively with their arms and voices. She jumped from the ground and grabbed for the first officer's gun, all in one motion. Had she looked me in the eyes midair? No matter—she never touched that gun. Not even close.

She was in midair when her wrist was grabbed. The officer dropped into a defensive stance while twisting Stacy's airborne body across the room, guiding her violently to the ground. The other two officers zip-tied her hands and feet like a baby calf at the rodeo. She didn't struggle. Not because she couldn't; she didn't want to. She didn't want to be here. Maybe she didn't want to be *here*. Maybe that was her attempt at suicide? Death by cop. She failed. They scooped her off the ground and carried her luau pig–style through the hall, down the stairs, and out into the paddy wagon. She was headed to the Germantown CRC, where she would be evaluated and more than likely sign herself in. Hopefully, sign herself in. Then she'd be pumped so full of drugs that she might have wished for the old days of Byberry. This was what she wanted, though. She couldn't really survive on the outside. She needed to be in some-body's care. Real care. Not the state-mandated thirty-four-dollar-a-day care. Not my mini-looney-bin care. Naw. She needed the big guns, and somewhere deep down inside, she knew it. Well, goddammit, she was gonna get it. Lucky bitch. We all know deep down inside what we need. We fight it, though, preferring to remain "normal." Why is it that we are called "crazy" when we ask for it? Ask for what we need. Stacy cried and apologized to me the whole way out. Thank God nobody from DPW was there. Thank God this was in front of my staff. If not, I might have asked to crawl into that paddy wagon with her. Maybe take a day or two off in the CRC, get some good meds in me, watch TV, not be responsible.

CRC is better than a Caribbean vacation. In Jamaica, you still got people harassing you to rent the Jet Skis or braid your hair or buy the jewelry because "I only make five dollars a month, and these drinks are included, and your wife wants to take a tour." Not in CRC: just TV and meds and food. Sounds like bliss. I gotta stay here and protect the license, though.

Sad that the only thing I could think of was my own

license. My safety blanket. Didn't want anyone or anything to jeopardize it. Didn't used to be that way. There was a time when I felt comfortable in the knowledge that doing a good job was all you had to do, but things had changed since the new regime of Mrs. Schitz had taken over. Now all I worried about was licensing and paperwork. The front door closed, and everyone looked at me. What do you say after that scene? How do I calm my troops, let them know it will all be all right?

"Who wants pizza?"

15

FRAGILE

Amoment of weakness can change the world forever. Many times, I fantasize about waking up in a quiet household. No arguments about hair choices or weather-appropriate clothing or breakfast consumption. Just quiet. I walk across the floor of my immaculate bedroom and turn on the lights. It's 5:30 a.m. I turn on *SportsCenter* with the volume at ten and ready myself for my jog in the bathroom. But just as I flush the toilet with the bathroom door wide open, *I wake up!* The sounds rush in. The crash of dishes, the barking dog, the hissing cat. Tweens arguing. It all rushes in, and I'm here, and I'm trapped, and I chose this. In a moment of weakness, couldn't we all envision leaving? Maybe they would all be better off without me. They certainly would be richer. What am I teaching them by simply waking every day and going through the motions? Those moments come and go for me.

Don't they come and go for you?

Ten p.m. I'm at a bar for couples' night with wifey and Ian and April. My phone rings. I'm on my third old-fashioned, and Ian seems funnier than usual. Even my wife is having a great time yapping to his wife, which is rare. Not that his wife isn't amusing, but my wife is picky with whom she hangs. Ya know, she gets tired of being the only black girl or the only couple that likes each other or the only people under fifty, so sometimes we just hang with each other, and that's fine, until you feel like killing each other. So to break up the monotony, you go on double dates, and the perfect couples are hard to find. Anyway, everything is going great. We're drinking and laughing and dreaming about the future, but then my phone rings. It's Amy, Colin's girl. Colin's sick. Very sick. He's had . . . a moment of weakness.

I don't recommend googling while driving, but everybody does it, just not as well as me, but ya know, we all got our talents. We live in the "now" generation. The "now" era. Remember when looking something up required the dreaded task of opening an encyclopedia? It seems like ancient fucking times now, like we should be making documentaries on that era for children to understand the struggle we went through. Back then, if someone asked you something that needed to be looked up, the most common response was, "Fuck that shit. It ain't that important." Thank God for Google. Within seconds, I am an expert on antifreeze ingestion—accidental and otherwise. My pseudo-educated by the internet yet knowledgeably informed opinion: *fuck!*

Colin looks terrible. Wires protrude from all orifices and undetermined points in a comical maze while his fidgeting, red-booted footies poke out of the grandma blankie. He is happy to see me, but the feeling isn't mutual. I can't help it. This guy was strong. This guy was my mentor . . . kind of. When I hung with him, I was in the presence of royalty. He was a rock star. Now look at him. The cocaine had so rotted his body and brain that he drank antifreeze? He had to try to kill himself? His kidneys had immediately failed. ARF, acute renal failure. No, I wasn't happy to see him. I was scared to fucking death. I sat next to him and tried to pretend everything was cool, but it was hard. It was impossible. It might have been easier if he were dead. Good thing I had the shades on. Maybe he didn't see the tears well up in my eyes: tears of fear and pain and regret. All this from a moment of weakness.

How many times have I had one? This life doesn't seem real, and I want it to end. That's what I think, at least. I want to push reset and redo everything. I love the end of *The Truman Show*. He pushes himself to the very limit. Risks everything to get where and what he wants. He ultimately finds that there is so much more. He breaks free. That's what we want, isn't it? That's what I want. Freedom. A suicide attempt is an attempt to break free. Death seems so free and easy. Truman gets to do it the way we all want to. One day, if I could peel away this world. Peel away the smiling neighbors and barking dogs and tree-lined streets and bluish-gray buildings and the winding streets leading to the same places for the same errands. I have been here so many times before. It's time for change. We yearn for it. A moment of weakness and you might seek it. Colin did. Now look at him.

Perhaps this is the director's warning to me. He sees me yearning for freedom. He sees me hopping on planes. Do these planes really fly? He sees me looking for change. Maybe Colin is in on it. Maybe this is a plot point in my reality TV show. When Truman climbs those stairs, I'm climbing right with him. Climbing out of this life. These choices. This world. Opening the door to a brand new, unencumbered future. In the end, the movie ends, though. And I'm still here. And Colin still has tubes stuck up his ass, sucking his blood out and recycling it through an oversize vacuum cleaner.

The same faces repeat themselves in the world. Do we have doppelgangers, or is the director running out of actors? I'm catching on, motherfucker. This is some bullshit. Do better. The nurses in Colin's room look familiar. Can this be real? My head starts swimming. I have to leave. Colin understands. I'm crying as I sprint through the hallways toward the street. The crisp air is welcome in my lungs because I feel like I'm suffocating. The air is sweet, and the street is empty.

My phone is in my hand. That old number gets dialed. My truck melts into the street and oozes through the night on its own as I head for a fix. Same shit. Different day.

A moment of weakness.

16

RIDGELINE

Puffy said he came here to live, not to die, so what did I come here for? I'm not really sure. Life has been easy. Too easy. I don't feel fully engaged, and maybe it's because I have never been challenged. For my survival, I mean. My clients have been challenged; they have been poor and abused and forgotten and exploited. And they don't care. They gave up a long fucking time ago. Some of them never even tried, maybe never could. Ah, the bliss they must feel not caring. Or at least that's my perception. But what about the rest of us? Those who are conscious. Those of us who are "sane." We are doomed to realize our insignificance and the ultimate goal of overcoming it. They're happily mired in the underbelly of society while we strive for greatness. For immortality. None of us wants to die. We believe by making a pile of money or kids or ourselves famous, we won't die.

But we will. One of these days . . . we will return to the essence, and none of this will matter.

Uncle Peter's funeral was on a hot Saturday afternoon. I'm not big on funerals. A bunch of decrepit people in tattered, ill-fitted clothing lying about an acquaintance long forgotten. More directly, they remind me of my end to come. I calculate how many years I have left. Am I really middle-aged already? Fuck. I'm not categorically young anymore. I thought I had more time to get this right. But life ain't no dress rehearsal. They raise the curtain, and you just gotta jump onstage.

Peter was a man's man. Owned real estate. Fixed cars. Fucked girls. Ya know, a man's man. I guess. He used to tell me my Chevy Avalanche was a Honda Ridgeline because . . . well, I don't fuckin' know why he would say that. True, they do look somewhat alike, but clearly they are different. If *similar* were the criteria, we could call both trucks an El Camino. But similar ain't what we're talking about, now, is it? And even if they are similar, I fucking told you this is an Avalanche. I mean, isn't that enough? OK! Avalanche, moth-erfucker! Not a fucking Honda! Maybe he was just focused on the big picture. Maybe I should be too.

Now Peter is lying there. Casket fresh. Unable to go back and call my truck by its proper name. Unable to do over. I wonder what he would do. I want to push reset. I would love to go back and use what I know now, but honestly, I would settle for just going back. More time. Never enough time.

Don't we all? I hope we all do. Or maybe I'm different. My employees are so happy, and I don't know why.

They don't make a lot of money. They aren't famous. They are rarely appreciated. Yet they seem happy. Sheila blasts church music in the kitchen while she has pots boiling with delicious food and a bank account full of nothing. Is this her passion? Did she always dream of providing nutritious meals for the mentally disabled? Medications for the mentally disabled? Appointment assistance for the mentally disabled? What will they leave when they die?

Peter left a lot of memories. He left a church full of love. One after another, his friends stood in testimony to his quirky character. They recanted stories of his ego and brashness and idiosyncrasies and how much they loved him because of and/or despite them all. Will I be remembered like that? Will anyone stand and testify? Not just give some bullshit lip service to me being a great guy, but really testify?

As the church fires up another hymn to celebrate Peter's life, I recall that a few years back, Philadelphia had three snowstorms hit within two weeks. The city was buried beneath four and a half feet of snow. SEPTA wasn't running. Schools were closed. In my business, there are no days off. My staff was being pushed to the limit. Miller stayed up forty-eight hours straight. Maybe that's when he was on coke. I can't remember . . . but whatever he did, he stayed up. I had to get Miller some relief, so I ventured out into the storm to retrieve workers from all over the city. This wasn't the first time. I had done it a few times early on in my career. For some reason, the calm of the empty streets struck me harder this time. It was just me and quiet and whiteness.

Sinclair is so happy to hop in my truck. He is so happy to come to work. Does his paycheck make him happy? I guess since I pay him in cash maybe it does. Sinclair is one of those illegals from Jamaica stealing your jobs. Stealing. Ha! Oh yeah, my door is overrun with Americans trying to wipe ass for $8.50 an hour. Yeah. Anyway, Sinclair is fucking happy. I mean, really happy. He bounds down the front stairs of his apartment building. Look at that shitty apartment building. Could I live there? Raise my family there? And be happy? His smile is ear to ear when he hops up into my truck. Does it occur to him that this truck is more than his yearly salary? Does he care? How is he so fucking happy?

As we maneuver, he is talking nonstop. Diarrhea of the mouth. Sinclair loves to tell me all about what's wrong at the building. The pipes that leak, the stove that quit, the staff that's lazy, the residents that do drugs. He is never able to corner me in the building . . . oh, that's why he is so fucking happy. He drones on and on while I'm trying to remember if I dropped any drug paraphernalia on the floor last night. I would hate to have to deal with that situation. What would I do? Deny . . . blame . . . kill. Yeah, it would feel good to kill Sinclair. He is so fucking annoying, jabbering on like this. And being so happy. He makes me feel ashamed. I am rich (relatively speaking) and successful (relatively speaking), yet he is so happy and content with his life. Is that the curse of intelligence? But above all else, he is right. The building is a mess. He should own the place, not me.

Uncle Peter's high school friends retell story after story up in the pulpit. Uncle Curtis slowly rises from his pew. He is a tall man with a shock of hair, thick glasses, and an offbeat gate. He meanders to the pulpit, and for the first time I can remember . . . he is crying.

Curtis married Abigail twenty-two years ago after both their former marriages crumbled. Abigail's first husband, George, was a truck driver hauling produce on the Eastern seaboard. During a run through North Carolina, he made a rest stop. He preferred to pull his semi to the far right, away from all the other drivers. Drivers had a habit of picking up passengers who liked to party and pilfer. He didn't want any trouble. After he retired to his sleeping quarters, he watched television until the television was watching him. Maybe that's why he never heard Vitelli and Mulligan sneak up on his rig from the nearby dense brush. Mulligan and Vitelli were two lifelong fuckups: one a meth addict, the other a pedophile. It honestly doesn't really matter which was which. Tonight, the dimwitted duo was fixing to steal some cargo for a quick flip. George probably thought he was dreaming when he first heard the lock on his rig crack. His big sad brown eyes probably snapped open when Tweedle Dee and Tweedle Dumb clumsily swung the enormous steel door open way too fast, and it hit the side of the payload with a loud clang. George no doubt spied the moonlight's reflection of his violated payload door as he carefully attempted to quiet the crunching of the gravel beneath his feet.

Clothed in only a wife beater, boxers, and slides, he made a determined attempt to protect the precious cargo. But why? Didn't he have insurance? Didn't his employer? Was there something in that payload that belonged to him or might have caused him embarrassment? What was George thinking? Too late. Vitelli's gun ignited the night sky from George's left flank. The piece-of-shit motherfucker had been standing guard in the bushes the entire time. George didn't have a chance. Abigail didn't have a husband.

Curtis had watched his first wife wither away from the ravages of cancer. Nobody knows what cancer is, but we damn sure know what it does. It kills. Every year we donate and walk and run, and people drop like flies anyway. Ain't no profit in the cure. Curtis's wife Lidya had been a statuesque ebony queen, the kind of woman with a sharp mind and tongue to match. Lidya was making a sizable income as a professor of economics at Virginia Tech when she took ill. It was a rapid decline. One day, her vivacious older frame was at the chalkboard and bending over coughing. The blood trickling out of the corner of her mouth betrayed the strength she tried to project. One of her students ran for help. The next thing Curtis knew, Lidya was in hospice. The curves that used to delight his eyes were snatched away and replaced with a skin-and-bone imposter. Who the fuck is this!? Probably wished for her to die sometimes. In between pureeing her food and sponging off her body, there wasn't much time for Curtis to grieve. Her blanket lay neatly across her body. She was so thin it was almost flat on the bed. Curtis had just finished injecting her dinner into her feeding tube and was turning the channel to *Monday Night Football*. She wouldn't care anyway. Suddenly, her whole body rose up. The blanket flopped off the bed, and her robe splayed open, revealing her once-beautiful bosom ravaged to a prunish decay. She gasped for air one last time and sat back down. At peace, finally.

I forgot what I was saying. This shit is all too sad, man. All this shit.

Anyway, I want people to dance at my funeral. RIP, "Ridgeline."

17

TICK-TOCK

Time keeps on slipping.

Did I hear Shelly right? 2011? Steve Jobs died in 2011? That's four fucking years ago. What the fuck is she talking about? He died last year, I thought. It's 2015. What the fuck is going on? I distinctly remember reading the reports of his death, his gradual demise from cancer. I know it was last year; no fucking way it was four years ago. No fucking way. Google. October 5, 2011. Fuck. I'm really losing track of time. This is not good.

It's always hard to concentrate in my continuing education classes. I mean, I have been an administrator for . . . twenty years. Shit. I'm old. It's especially tough today because the slide she has hanging behind her is of Steve Jobs. Cerebral. Successful. Dead. 2011. I'm really confused and can't ask anybody in the class. I mean, obviously, he died in 2011. It wouldn't be up there if he hadn't; she's boring but accurate. I'm beginning to panic. The room is vibrating. Could I have really misplaced four years? Is that even possible? What did I do? Cocaine mostly, I guess. Shame. Shelly drones on. Today's topic is hiring the right people. Great. The *right* person is the person who says yes to washing ass for five bucks an hour. "Will you clean shit for five bucks an hour? Yes? You're hired!" Shelly has another opinion.

Hiring the right person is about approaching your interview with a strategy. What kind of person are you looking for? Patient? Self-motivated? Tidy? Fastidious? Willing to wipe ass. In order to find them, you need to approach the interview like a battle. Make them wait for you. Pretend to be the secretary and see how they act in the lobby. Do they complain about their last job? Walk them through the building. Do they interact with the clients? Does a humongous veiny penis scare them? Conduct a group interview and pretend to be one of the group. How do they treat their fellow interviewees? Do they plug their phone up to keep their battery charged in case of emergency? If your assistant secretly calls their phone in the middle of your interview, will they answer?

But most importantly, in my humble opinion, will they wipe ass for five bucks an hour?

Shelly lets us go a little early. It's December 2, and she has Christmas shopping to do and applications to assist her son in filling out. He's an avid hunter and doesn't understand that Northeastern liberal academics have issues with grown men hiding in bushes and shooting Bambi from a safe distance of two hundred yards away for the fuck of it. So I get to go take care of some errands before leaving town to visit my kids. Oh shit, I forgot to mention my wife left.

How long can you expect someone to watch you destroy your life? There really wasn't anything I could say. She moved out, took my kids and half my cash. Now we were just the typical American family. Well, not really, she always fucking left. She always fucking came back. Not sure why. Love, I guess. After a while, she just couldn't take it anymore. Enough was enough, right? She just couldn't love anymore. All out of love. I wasn't devastated. I was relieved. I wanted her to leave. They deserved better than what I had to give. Better than what I was willing to give. She packed the kids and the suitcases and *poof!* She was gone. She should have left years ago. Stayed too long. The first time I came in sniffling at 5:00 a.m. The first time I had those paranoid delusions. The rehab center we called warned her. Told her I was a liar. Told her we were all liars. I wasn't lying; I was broke. I didn't have $20,000 to spend on treatment, and so I had hoped the demons and the voices would just go away. They warned her. She didn't listen. She stayed. She's a saint. But then she wasn't able to handle the descent. I don't blame her. I wanted her to go. Since then, it has all been a blur. An eye-squinting-from-painful-headaches blur.

I shake the cobwebs off and look up, and here I am. Still alone.

I'm beginning to try and piece together what happened this week, so I can start with a baseline on how I lost four years. There was a terrorist attack, the Eagles blew the game, and the city sent me a notice that I owed thirty-eight grand. Could be any week. Fuck. Shit. Is. Getting. Real. Actually, I'm beginning to panic. I decide to pull into Andy's Diner. It just so happens that my favorite sports talk show is broadcasting live. Watching them broadcast is weird. It doesn't seem real. Every day, while I trudge through the dreck that is my life, I listen to these guys. Not just listen. Argue. Talk. Communicate. I laugh with them, reminisce, and get angry. In person, you can't really do any of that. I mean, you can nod and chuckle a bit, but when Seth Joyner starts to talk about the days of yesteryear when the Eagles defense dominated the NFC under Buddy Ryan, you can't get misty eyed and stare out the window—especially when you already don't fit in, wearing your houndstooth trench coat and Goorin Brothers hat. They already think you're a fag; sitting there is fun but depressing. These guys aren't my friends. In the truck they are, but really, these guys aren't my friends. Come to think of it, who is?

Who do I talk to and spend most of my time with? Who do I lean on now that my wife is gone? Sure, I have people who call me for money; I have people who ask my advice. I have my radio relationship, but who would I call if I needed something *real*? Who would help me? Who are my *friends*? I am responsible for the lives of thirty-nine people plus, like, ten staff. Who feels responsible for me, though? I reached out to several friends lately for business ideas. All my friends are in business with each other—some manufacture clothing, others produce music, others write TV shows. I don't even remember when they started. Some of them never told me they moved and got married to famous people. I had to find out watching TMZ and pretend I was in the loop when my mother asked. Where had the time gone, and why did it take my friends from me? My family from me?

I'm beginning to panic a bit. All my friends shut me down. They won't say no; they just don't do it. They don't fill out that form or answer that email or text; they all treat me like I have it made with this personal care shit. Like, that's what I do, but that's not what I want to do. I want to do anything else. I want to write or network or wear a suit or file a report or flip a house or any fucking thing . . . but this.

The employees aren't my friends. They like me (or don't), but they aren't my friends. I am the asshole who signs their checks. They tolerate me. I guess I'm a better boss than most, but they don't like me. Maybe Miller does? I don't know if it's for real, though. It's lonely now. My people hang up with me and continue with their exciting lives— going in and out of meetings and traveling for business and golfing for work—and leave me behind. My children are growing. I wanna cry out or maybe just cry, but nobody is listening.

I'm losing my mind, "friend"! I misplaced four years!

I call Carl. Carl will listen.

Carl answers. He feels me. I am not the only one. It isn't the monotony of my life or the crushing weight of my failed dreams that have caused the time to slip; it's the cosmic discord. Carl lives in California now. Carl is fucking losing it. Fucking. Losing. It. As I said earlier, there was a terrorist attack this week. Another terrorist attack. Syed Rizwan Farook and Tashfeen Malik—a married couple in San Bernardino—amassed an armory of weapons including assault rifles, handguns, body armor, pipe bombs, and thousands upon thousands of rounds of ammunition. For reasons only known to them, they dropped off their six-month-old baby at Grammy's house and proceeded to murder the attendees of the annual holiday party at Farook's job. Maybe it was terrorism; maybe he didn't like his Secret Santa. I don't know, but it has affected Carl . . . deeply. Carl is wired and talking with a panic. We share some similar worldviews on the government (and an embarrassing history of drug use), so I thought he would be the perfect ear to vent to about my newfound loss of time. He is . . . kind of. He has a theory: I am not the only one. I am not alone in my loss of time. He, too, feels it; San Bernardino feels it. The world is spinning out of control. I had noticed his Facebook posts becoming more and more erratic, pleading for someone to stop the madness. It's not that I disagree with him; I am just not one to voice my every thought on social media. Revolutionary rhetoric doesn't seem to jibe with pictures of my dog. Fuck, I can't even remember what kind of dog I have. It's getting worse. Maybe Carl is right.

He believes that we are living in the end of days. The frequency of black men murdered by police, terrorists wantonly slaughtering the innocent, mysterious diseases attacking our population, drought and war coupled with government leaders arguing nonsensically on both sides of every issue with no solution in sight have him scared. I find myself defending my right to singular insanity, but he will have none of it. I'm not going insane; I'm aware. Whether consciously or not, I am feeling the "vibes of the world, bro." Carl has been living in LA too long.

When I say I misplaced four years, I want him to tell me it's the drugs catching up with me. Sobriety is hard to deal with. You have to face the carnage you wreaked on yourself. Rehab ruined my life. But he doesn't agree. He tells me the world is still. Too still. The energy we all share—whether you call it the cosmos or God or Allah or Yahweh or what-ever—has been permanently altered. There is no way for me not to feel it.

Goddammit!

Did he even hear me? Maybe that's why I can't remember the last few years; I'm not real. Or I died. Scott

Weiland just died of an overdose; maybe I did too. I am just a spirit roaming the earth, searching for peace for my soul. I should have gone to church. We hang up, and I continue through the streets. Am I calloused because this is a seemingly everyday occurrence? Maybe I am desensitized by the inundation of horror the American viewer is subjected to, or maybe I am used to death. Used to stillness—after all, my job is to watch over the forgotten. Therefore, I have been forgotten too. So whether terrorists murder fourteen people singing "Deck the Halls" in San Bernardino, or Mrs. Walker dies in the middle of the hallway at 3:00 a.m., and the obese coroner can't get the gurney upstairs, and I'm forced to help him awkwardly carry her lifeless body down the narrow stairwell while her husband looks on crying, the world will keep spinning. The oceans will continue to brew life. The wind will blow, and the seasons will change. And isn't that the rub? The slap in everyone's face—that ultimately, none of us matter that much. In the grand scheme of things, we aren't that important, so maybe my friends aren't my friends, and maybe my business is a nightmare. Maybe you have amassed a fortune and live in a big house and drive a fancy car, and your wife has perfect tits and abs. At the end of the day, everyone else will keep on living without you, and when the human race finally ends, the earth will continue to spin. Then, out of the primordial ooze, some new species will crawl. Maybe I will be one of them. Reincarnated. A second chance. This time, I will get it right. No personal care.

Cockapoo? Labradoodle? *Yorkie poo!* That's what I have! A yorkie poo named Lenny.

Yeah, I remember.

For now.

18

MIAMI

This guy's house will make you cry. This guy's house will make you reevaluate your whole fuckin' life. I haven't seen it yet, but I believe what Abayomi is saying. Today, I'm in Miami. I can't afford to be here, but that never stopped me from buying hundreds of dollars of cocaine and stuffing it up my nose, so why should I start being fiscally responsible now? Besides, it's better than Philly. Despite the rat-trap airline crew hotel I'm staying at, it's an upgrade in settings. Trips are cool that way. One minute, you're in the shit . . . and then you are somewhere else. Insert fast-paced movie montage moment.

Last week I was knee deep in personal care. And anger and sorrow and pain and complaints . . . and . . .

and . . .

and . . .

Now I'm at a dingy bar in my shitty Miami hotel listening to airline pilots discuss the lack of Dodge Caravan space in their garage. People still drive those things? I really am not of this world. I realized it last week in Restaurant Depot. That's the place where restaurants shop. Clever, right? I noticed all the people buzzing along doing their jobs. Living their lives. Droning. Making the honey. Dreaming of their fifteen-minute smoke break. And there's my contrasting mood. No, I'm not of this world. They bee along in this warehouse: no sunlight, no hope, no dreams, no clocks. Time doesn't matter here. Only commerce. Buying and selling. Running on their wheels. Faster, faster, and maybe you can outrun your impending death. Maybe, just maybe, if you run fast enough . . . trying to outdo each other. Look at my business grow. Two stores now. My wife has new tits. We bought a beach house. Our kids are backpacking through Sweden. Friend me. Envy me. Fuck me. I dunno. I just don't get it anymore. I'm spoiled. I know it. I have everything anyone wants, but I feel it's all a sham. The curtain needs to be pulled away. Why do you want to climb up to that shelf to help me get more toilet paper? Fuck that toilet paper. Ahmad calls me beloved. Weird. I hate Ahmad. No, I like Ahmad. He is content. I am jealous. He makes a shitty wage in a shitty job and he seems . . . content. I can't seem to find that. These material possessions are adding up to zero. I need this getaway. I'm gonna drop this load at the building and go to Miami. That will make everything better. Right.

Anyway, that's me in Miami, hating everyone around me, only with more sunshine and going outside. The soulless pilots sit around at the roach motel, drinking their drinks and talking to each other. Just living, I suppose. Maybe they're just ignorant to the fact that they're distracted and afraid. They don't know anything. Or maybe it's just me.

The bartender is friendly. "Calls you sweetie and sugar" friendly. "Refreshes your bar snacks without you asking" friendly. "I'm sure she has gone upstairs with a middle-aged divorced pilot" friendly. The blackness of her hair betrays her age, though. She is desperately clinging to her youth. Poorly. Her jeans are fastened way too high on the belly that long ago abandoned those children in the Midwest town she escaped. Her cigarette breath wafts methodically toward me. It lingers in the air only to be trapped by the matted green carpet stapled to the floor and walls. She is probably proud of her shitty Christmas decorations. Shame that New Year's Eve is coming. She will be forced to untangle the tinsel for safekeeping. The drinks she makes the pilots are generous yet watered down. Her machine-gun conversation skills mow down the bellied up. No different than most. Most don't listen; they just wait for their turn to talk. I worry that the conversation skills of our youth will be destroyed by their addiction to social media and electronics, but the truth of the matter is the devices they hold so dear are simply a distraction to an affliction that has long plagued mankind: loneliness. We are lonely. Eight fucking billion of us on the planet, yet we are lonely. Our evolution has led us there—or here, rather. Once our prehistoric ancestors roamed the earth proudly, killing and fucking anything and everything. Slowly, we developed intelligence and emotions, and our fates were sealed. We started to feel.

Loneliness. It's not real. Instead of instincts, we had feelings. We yearned for the touch of another, yearned to belong to a group. And so we congregated and started families and built rules and created gods to make us feel safe and warm and not like bacteria oozing over the surface of a ball of fire hurtling through space aimlessly. Billions of years of evolution, but here we sit at the bar, pretending to care about the bartender's brother Luke "who receives thirteen hundred dollars per month, but then gets another seven hundred dollars, so at any rate, he receives more than two thousand dollars per month, and he is thirty-one years old now, so when Momma, bless her heart, says don't give him another dime, she means it—like, not even in line at McDonald's or at 7-Eleven. Nuh-uh, nope, not another dime ... you need a refill, sweetie?"

Yeah, just waiting for our turn to talk. Afraid to be alone. Afraid of silence. Stillness. We have to be doing something. "What brings you to Miami?" A plane. I don't know. I didn't want to blow my brains out in Philly is the reality of the situation but probably an unsavory way to converse with strangers. Fucking Miami. New York and LA's bastard child.

I am finished. The conversation, the people watching, and the drink. The lobby is clinging to yesteryear. The marble floors have dulled over time while the chandeliers have ceased to deserve the replacement of all their bulbs. The furniture gave up providing proper support years ago. It sags to the dimensions of someone who left a long time ago. It kind of looks like it's waiting for them to return. Sad. Lonely. There aren't many little kids here. The real action is down closer to South Beach, where we will meet Abayomi at the "house" later. Here, the one kid I see is on the elevator with me. He sees the ragged wood floors, the torn carpet, the ancient buttons missing numbers, and the space above him where the fluorescent bulb should be. He doesn't care that his family is poor. He is happy. Be like a child. Be happy.

The 1970s asbestos popcorn tile. The chipped gold mirror slightly askew. The moist plywood nailed to the ceiling like a medieval wound covering. My chest is getting tight. The doc says it's psychosomatic. Says I'm too young to have a heart attack. Only stress. Too young to have a heart attack? What the fuck does that mean? There's no logic or guarantee in that. They strapped me up to an EKG and had me running and breathing, and after a few hours and blips and beeps on the screen, he says I'm fine. Just stress. But. My. Chest. It's still tight. The smell of mold in the hallway is invading my nostrils. My head is getting light. Thankfully, I make it into my room and shut the door behind me. Wifey stands naked in the middle of the drab hotel room. Not bad for a mother of two. I thought she left me. I'm losing it. All the same, her smile brings me out of the depression. How does she do that? How can she be so happy here? In this place, while her cousin stays down in South Beach at that ritzy hotel with her rich doctor boyfriend eating fucking caviar and salad and Oreos. Because she isn't really here. That's how. As I fall backward onto the bed, I finally breathe. I hadn't noticed I was holding my breath until now. Maybe that's why my chest was so tight. Maybe.

At dinner that night, I meet more of Abayomi's rich friends. I mean, fuck! Am I the only loser on the planet? What do a doctor, a senior vice president, and an investment banker have in common? More money than me. Is that what it's all about, Earl? Money? Nice hotels? Fancy cars and trips and clothes? No. Not really. It's vocation. I envy their vocation. I envy their reason for being. They get up every day with a purpose. "My name is Abayomi, and today, I will go into the ER and save somebody's fucking life." Maybe he hates his job too. Maybe he can't stand the sight of diseased vaginas and gunshot wounds and vomiting kids. I don't know, but they all seem so focused and content. Me, I'm just floating around not knowing where to go, and regardless of how I feign normalcy, I can't seem to reach the ground.

Tonight is the pregame to New Year's Eve, but the bill is a fucking monster. Twelve hundred dollars. Fuck me. I got the $300 but fuck. The banker laughs at the bill and says, "At least Abayomi got the $10K hookup for tomorrow night." The hookup. Great, I need a hookup; these drinks are expensive here in Miami and I—Wait, *ten thousand dollars*? Did this motherfucker say ten thousand dollars? What the hell? I guess Abayomi sees the stress on my face. When nobody is paying attention, he leans in and tells me he got me. He didn't expect me to pay that shit. That's a good doc. When I was a kid, Davis Niles's dad had a great job on Wall Street, and his mom never worked. One day his dad got up and did his usual routine: dressed, breakfast, and off to work. He got on the train, and Nicky never saw him again. He went to buy the *Philadelphia Bulletin* and dropped dead in the middle of 30th Street Station.

He was too young to have a heart attack.

It was only stress.

19

HONG KONG

The one on Wynnefield? What the fuck do you mean, the one on Wynnefield? You didn't say a goddamn thing about Wynnefield. You said the LKF Hotel. I booked the LKF Hotel. The LK fucking F Hotel, man. We spoke months ago. Three fucking months ago, and now the night before I fly to a foreign country—all the way around the goddamned world like fucking Magellan or some shit, twenty-six hours of flight—now you are on my goddamned phone telling me there is not one but two LKF Hotels in Hong Kong. And I booked the wrong one. When did you come upon this information, pray tell? I mean, you only go to Hong Kong fifty fucking times a year, you fucking idiot.

I love Dan. I mean really love Dan. He is everything I want to be. Tall, confident, handsome, but Jesus, he is stupid. Well, maybe not stupid; maybe he just doesn't care. More than likely didn't think I would really go. Three months ago, I got the crazy idea to take my ex-wife to Japan. When I first met her twenty years ago, she was fascinated with Japan. She has Japanese flashcards, and she bought Rosetta Stone (it was Chinese, and she never opened it), but you get the point. She loved Japan. Maybe not so much the geography but . . . dammit, I'm digressing.

I call up my boy Dan, who works for a major shoe company, for some advice. Gonna rekindle this relationship with a trip for her birthday, and who better to ask than Dan? The company sends him all over the world and especially to Asia. He says don't go to Japan. Apparently, Japan is not the place to visit for your first time in Asia. "Too Asian," he says. Even gets his coworker who lived there for two years on the phone to tell me her opinion. She is half Korean, and it was too Asian for her. Umm, a little self-hate, honey? OK, OK, I got it. The verdict: Hong Kong.

So he gives me the breakdown. Starts with the accommodations. LKF Hotel. I see it on my travel website. They are running a deal. Flight and stay is, like, a four grand total for the both of us. Shiiiiit. Hong Kong, here I come! Bring a suit. Stay up late. Blah, blah, blah.

Three months later . . . oh yeah, make sure you booked the one on Wynnefield.

I leave tomorrow, asshole. Thanks.

My ex-wife is great. I'm sitting in our Jeep about to cry. I don't give a fuck; it ain't the first time she has seen me cry. I have broken down many times fighting this demon inside me. She may smoke too much pot and not clean the house and yell at the kids and not watch sports and like reality TV and not know shit about politics and . . . what the fuck was I saying? Oh yeah, but she supports me. She sees me upset. The conversation with Dan had gotten loud. "No worries," she says. "As long as we're together," she says.

"Now, that's some good dick," I say.

She laughs.

With me.

I hope.

Nothing is going to stop me. It's 11:00 p.m., and I'm running errands for this godforsaken business, but nothing can bring me down. Not the nefarious characters populating the Save-A-Lot parking lot. Not the creepy guy selling light-up flowers in the aisle. Not even the ignorant fucking bitch texting and tossing my products into my cart, only to have to rescan them because if you hadn't noticed, you little twat . . . I have multiples. Nope, nothing is gonna get me upset.

OK, maybe this bitch texting on her phone is upsetting me a little. Who the fuck is she? An international arms financier moonlighting as an overnight cashier at a discount grocery store in Germantown? When did we all become so fucking important that we can't tear ourselves away from our goddamned phones and social media? There is a war going on. I truly believe corporate America has waged war on the populace. They want to enslave us through "smart-phones" and apps and TV and digital information. The cashier's eyes are glazed, and her mouth is slightly ajar. She looks mentally disabled a bit. I swear I can see her brain synapses firing slower and slower. I want to tell her. I want to shake her, but . . . fuck this bitch. Every man for himself tonight.

In the morning, I'm flying to motherfucking Hong Kong. And this whore will still be here ignoring customers and texting her twin in ignorance about solutions for her weave tangle or cash-and-carry outfit dilemma. I dunno. Fuck it. I'm a terrible person, I guess.

The next morning we arrive at the airport super early—like three hours early. I'm anal about very little, but getting to the airport on time is top of the list. It annoys the shit out of my family. They take joy in teasing me as we traverse security lines and terminals through the airport, eons before our flight. They pretend to run on the automatic sidewalk, mocking my concerned pace, juxtaposed with our immense lead time to takeoff. It's one of the few times they "gang" up on me. I love it. Sidebar: How lazy are we that we can't walk? I mean, we aren't going up a hill. It's a fucking hallway, for God's sake.

Thankfully, we dropped the kids off last night at my

parents'. They would have been an absolute nightmare to take to Hong Kong or get up and out the door this morning. Kids are the ultimate narcissists. They don't give a shit about anything but themselves. They come home from school and throw their bullshit all over the front of the house, eat all the goddamn cereal, leave the bowls on the counter, go into the TV room, and argue over what channel to switch the TV to—although it's really fucking obvious I'm watching ESPN. I only stepped out of the room to change a load of laundry . . . *their* laundry!

Damn, I'm gonna miss them.

The plane is huge: Airbus A350. I am not sure when you are reading this, but at the present time (like when I'm writing this), that fucker is state of the art. This particular plane is probably only six months old. That's crazy. And it's luxurious. The crew are all beautiful and handsome, and their uniforms are designer. The plane opens up onto what looks like a bar. A bar? Oh baby. This is gonna be the greatest trip ever. Oh shit, the seats. The seats are beds. Beds, man! Mile-High Club, here we . . . cum? The pretty Asian flight attendant is smiling, *and* her mouth is moving. Is she talking to me? My ex-wife is right behind me; honey, wait until she falls asleep at least. Suddenly, the volume of the world is turned back on. The rush of sound drags me out of my daydream.

"Please continue to your right . . ."

Oh. OK.

So I'm not up here with the bar thingy or the beds or the hot towels and shrimp. How long did they say the flight was? Twenty-six hours? Where is that? Argh. Regular seats. Shoulda bought first class. Oh well. Complimentary drinks and dinner and fully reclining seats. Hey, it could be worse. I could be flying on US Air. They fucking suck. I wouldn't want my worst enemy to endure their service. Evil. They should rename themselves Evil Airlines. I think American Airlines would sue, though.

Hong Kong was interesting. The sheer volume of people, their largely homogeneous appearance. The street vendors grilling increasingly difficult-to-recognize animal parts for consumption. Whose consumption? Ours or theirs? Never mind. The buildings leaned toward the street, threatening to collapse from the weight of the souls piled on top of one another. It was busy and dirty and different and the same—like going to New York's Chinatown and finding that it had overtaken all of Manhattan. It smelled rotten. The air was foul and stale from cigarettes and garbage and tourism. Not everywhere—we did find a secret brunch spot by following wealthy-looking white kids into an elevator. We had tired of the stomach-turning soup options at the local McDonald's and had ventured out. Here we were. One-hundred-dollar-per-person brunch. The bartender took an immediate liking to us. Did he think we were famous or just crazy? Twenty-six hours away from home.

We are all crazy.

Nothing exciting happened in Hong Kong. Nothing. We walked a lot.

Fuck it.

Who cares?

Motherfuckers take flight for granted. They don't see it as magic anymore. According to NATCA, at any given point in time, there are roughly five thousand planes criss-crossing the airways above the United States, an estimated sixty-four million flights a year. Sixty-four million. That's just the US. Extrapolate to all the Americas. The whole planet. Motherfuckers just don't see it as any big fucking deal. Those silver tubes of thousands of hours of engineering and labor and testing, streaking through the sky. All started by two hick brothers in North Carolina, or so I'm told. We all stand in line and complain about the line and taking our shoes off and screaming babies and where's the food and we stare at our screens because we can't bear the boredom and close our windows and schedule our flights so we can sleep . . .

and . . .

and . . .

and . . .

Damn. We forgot it's magic. I want to feel the g-forces press me into my seat and my eyeballs exposed to the point of redness because they can't close. I want my lips to flap like in the cartoons I used to watch many years ago, but instead, I sit in my seat . . .

And then I wind up home. The reality is jarring. Scarring, really. Yes, I traveled by plane.

But I don't feel like I went anywhere.

We get home, and I can kind of hear my wife (ex-wife?) on the phone. Everything is hazy. Not jet lagged, just can't quite process this reality. What once was, is not. Hong Kong. Now Ardmore. I see her laughing. I'm laughing too. Texting, calling. Posting. We can't sleep. She turns on a reality show in which the participants are rappers. Old rappers. Their careers have a short half life, but with reality TV, they can revive them. They get a second act. The two old rappers are trying to make a comeback, but the young producer hitmaker empire builder is telling them they have no shot. Twenty years of music, and he is telling them they need to quit. Well, what the fuck else are they supposed to do? They didn't get this far working on their backup plan. They didn't fucking need to get degrees; they just needed to free their minds and believe in themselves. And they rose to heights they didn't think possible. Created their own lane. Became gods and, yes, slaves too.

And after all that, this . . . baby—infant, man-child in oversize, overdarkened glasses with chains draping everywhere—is telling them to quit. They thank him and leave. I want them to kick his ass and hold on to their careers with every ounce of strength they have, but they just thank him and leave. That night, they are in the park, and they turn on their boombox and their mics, and they perform. The people stop, and they stare, and they smile. These two don't perform for the money or the fame. They perform for each other and the fans. They perform for this force that is within them. Something that would not be denied drove them toward this. It never promised them anything but ended up giving them everything. They don't care what that baby says; they know who they are. What they are. I cry for them. For me. I want to hear that voice telling me to "just do it." I want to tap into that force. I want to have a second act. I want to be . . . alive.

But instead, I am back here in Philadelphia, and it's morning again. I'm in my office, and Carmen is yipping about something. She is a cute little girl. Very young. I'm sad for her. She has no dreams. Her mouth is moving, but my mind is somewhere else. The new lady we admitted is upstairs, and something else is going on. I'm floating above the desk looking at Carmen. We both have no dreams. We leave the office and rush up the stairs. Why are we rushing? Nobody is going anywhere. I am not a doctor. I won't perform CPR, so why the rush? I see the new lady; she seems fine to me. Why is everybody up here tripping? Their eyeballs convey fear; they are looking past me. In the family room on the floor, Mary is laid out. Dying? Not Mary. Not my little "weeble-wobble." The paramedics arrive; there is a flurry of activity. I still can't shake the fog. The new lady wants to meet me. She is pleasant enough. A former benefits administrator for a pharmaceutical firm who may have had a stroke, and now years later—despite eating right and exercise and attending church, saving puppies and greeting her fucking asshole neighbors with a smile—she ended up here. In a wheelchair . . . and a diaper. She scares me. She could be me. One day.

All of us live in fear, hurtling through space, wasting time, worrying about the diaper years. Saving and planning and fearing the diaper years. The commercial on TV with the green road that leads you to retirement and the other one with the orange squirrels that tell you to save your nuts for the future are turning us into robots. Wake, shit, consume, repeat. Maintaining a healthy amount of fear in us. Fear of us. They never tell us to dream; they program us to die. Spend your money and wait to die.

I don't want to give you the wrong impression. Those two rappers were millionaires. I checked. They had plenty of money and were making more money from that stupid reality show than 85 percent of the US population. I just found it interesting—no, inspiring. They weren't rapping because they wanted money. They were rapping because they needed to make music. There is something inside them that is bigger than fear. It drives them to create and perform and live beyond the confines of the box they want us in. I wanted that feeling. That drive. That inspiration. It's like when I was a kid and I doubted the existence of God, and so I challenged *Him* (Sexist little prick, right?) to kill a pigeon and drop it at my feet. I wanted that surety of myself that the faithful have, the confidence that the successful have, that thing . . . that . . .

Magic.

It didn't happen, though now I still walk around scared that one day a dead bird will randomly drop at my feet.

Fear.

20

CIMEX LECTULARIUS

Good night. Sleep tight. Don't let the bedbugs bite. Sounded innocuous enough when I was a kid. Never really gave it a second thought, to be honest. It's something my mom would say before she closed my door. I wouldn't go to sleep anyway. Had my flashlight ready and a novel under the covers. My mom would double back every so often, just to keep me honest. She thought it was cute. Don't let them bite. *Let*, as though we had a choice. Just saw a sign warning against the Zika virus at the airport. Same advice. Don't let the mosquitos bite. Just to be clear, when your baby is born with three eyeballs and no mouth from a disease that didn't exist two years ago, it ain't our fault. No no no no. Despite the fact we probably manufactured it in a lab or brought it back from our incessant space exploration, just to be clear: we told you not to *let* them bite you. You've been warned.

Look at them sitting there, smiling at me. At us. Their virtual-reality faces glowing from the screen. Invading my morning. I just want to get my coffee, read the news, and go to work. I don't bother attempting to roll over on my wife anymore. We have become like those wrinkled-up Florida couples, only with fewer liver spots. The headlines attack my senses. My day is altered. Why do I even fucking bother? It's not as if something different happened. The news is on repeat: police, fire, death, war, money, fame. Fear and consumption.

Zika. What the fuck is Zika? The CDC is telling me that some nasty motherfucker in Texas just caught Zika from some dirty-dick piece of shit from Venezuela. Three hundred million people in the country, and somehow the CDC knows this one motherfucker and her Latin lover. I don't know how these things get reported. You know how many people go to ER daily? How did they find out? Was her pussy glowing? Did his dick fall off? Did he walk into the ER with his dick in his hand? Then what the fuck made them test for Zika? That's an STD? There's gonorrhea, chlamydia, AIDS . . . and maybe something else . . . crabs . . . there's crabs. There ain't no Zika. I know; I've been burned twice. Shit hurts like a motherfucker.

A quick search of Zika on the internet produces enough responses to make you say, "Holy fuck! We are all going to die." The reality, of course, is that regardless of Zika, we all are still, in fact, going to die—a fact that seems lost on us as we stare into our screens and pray for hope. Easy for God to save us from terrorists, poverty . . . and Zika.

Holy shit. When did Zika become this huge problem? Where the fuck have I been? All these websites and news agencies are talking about Zika. I start reading this shit and fuuuuuck . . . Zika is spread through mosquitoes. Damn, I hate those things. Can't we just kill them? Did the Venezuelan guy fuck a mosquito? Would that be considered cheating on my wife? What wife?

Calm yourself, man. Pull it together. What's this Zika all about? Oh God. Oh no, it's incurable? What do they mean, *incurable*? Oh wait. Right. Everything is. These bastards haven't cured shit since polio, and even that's making a comeback (insert face of pharma exec). Ain't no profits in "the cure." OK, OK, OK. Nervous now. Sweating and late for work. Jesus fucking Christ. It's spring. How do I protect my kids from Zika? What are the symptoms? OK, OK, umm, "fever, rash, joint pain, and red eyes." Oh God. Oh no . . . wait, what? Fever, rash, joint pain, and red eyes. What the fuck is that? Sounds like the flu. Or a cold. Or my Aunt Mandy.

Dammit, they got me again.

Back in my city. The City of Brotherly Love. Back in Germantown. Historic. Iconic. Yet deplorable. Defeated. Dead. Can't wait to leave. The night before, I had dinner with my parents alone. Hadn't done that in a while. My mother and I argued. Playfully, as usual. I admit it, I was the one who started the argument, but she didn't back down . . . never does.

It all started when I told her about my latest endeavor. I am going to produce a documentary. It's what I went to school for. Received a full scholarship for. I have a story to tell. The pastor at the church in LA saw it in me. He said so when he saw me. Of course, they are all hippies running around there feeling the "vibrational frequencies," but I feel them too. And I believe him. I do have a story to tell. I am observant. I am intelligent. And I see now that I have mommy issues. Deep-seated, unrepented mommy issues. My desire to please her has clouded my vision and shaped most of my decisions. The saddest part is that the times I have been most happy were when I didn't do what she thought I should. Didn't do what I thought I should. Unfortunately, those decisions didn't ultimately make me a lot of money. And that is how she judges everything. By money.

And then I wake up in my bed. It's like that for me. Huge swaths of unaccounted time. I went to college for four years and only remember two classes. *Two*. Not my econ and English class, but literally two classes. Like a random econ class on a Monday, my swim test, first day of statistics and . . . that's it. Is that the way it's supposed to be? Hurtling through space, just rampaging across experiences? Kori remembers everything. Everybody. He showed me a picture of a pop star, who I apparently once knew. Until then, I didn't realize that we had been friends for such a long time. We were.

My bed. The ceiling stares back at me. Blankly. I feel the fibers of the sheets move across my skin, and I swear it's them. Who? Bedbugs, that's who. My building is infested with them. Insane. Not the people. Well, yes, the people, but that's not what I'm referring to. The level of infestation is insane. Bugs everywhere. They are unstoppable. A nocturnal horde of bloodsucking diminutive demons immune to pesticides. Insane. Are we all simply going to pretend? The city is overrun with them; my business certainly is. There is a fucking epidemic in Philadelphia, and nobody seems to give a fuck. Well, except DPW. Yes, our old friends DPW. The bane of my existence, the finger in my ass. DP fucking W. They care. They arrive on site just as dinnertime is ending. Just in time to see Miller clear the table after mopping the floor without washing his hands in between. Classic Miller. Thanks. Their faces crinkle a bit. They can't help revealing that revulsion. It's honest. Visceral. True. I'm not in the mood for this. But when am I ever?

Two inspectors, one me. Zero fucks. Look at my face. They know I don't care. Can they see the despair in me? Can they hear my mental ramblings of escape? Their mouths move, but it's hazy inside this room. And I can't see. I can't hear. I breathe in deeply as we are exiting the office and heading upstairs. Wipe that stupid smile off your face, Earl. You look like an idiot. We all go through this world faking smiles and contentment and success, hoping that someone believes, but in honesty, when all of us are so fucked up, I wonder why we care. The inspectors smile back as they rummage through this human garbage pile. These leftover wretches.

The thought of them closing me down used to scare me, but now it doesn't. Oh no, I am actually excited. I'm thinking of the possibilities. Dreaming, actually.

The door latch snapped into the backset, shattering my peace. I was snatched back in time like a jilted lover using H. G. Wells's time machine. Suddenly, it was two years before, and I was wired. I was walking into the den at 5:00 a.m., desperately trying to avoid detection by my wife . . . and my children. The snot in my nose ran down my lip, and I licked it off to savor the tart juices of my lover . . . the demon that had taken my soul. Head pounding and eyes wide, convinced that "her" henchmen were hiding behind the couch, beyond that door, inside the shower. The paranoia had reached perilous heights. I made my way to the couch and turned on . . . anything. The thought in my mind was to have enough background noise to hide my nefarious activity. Yes, at 5:00 a.m., I wasn't done. No. I was just getting started.

Then, the next door neighbors' discourteous beast howled, fracturing my trance. Damn. This is what it's become: nothing more than stumbling memories. "People, places, and things," they told me. The legitimacy of that statement was uncanny. I am an addict. No, for real. Like a bona fide real-deal addict. When I stopped, I thought that was the end. Quitting is an action verb, however. Never more factual than when describing this process because it never stops.

Cocaine versus me was a long war. I lost many battles along the way. I've won the war—well, the cease-fire—but have been left permanently scarred by the ordeal. The inability to drive through the city or enter any restaurant or bathroom or walk into my own family room is a heavy tax to pay. When I do, my PTSD is often triggered. Sometimes it's minor, like a glance at a shelf or a sigh pulling into a parking lot. Other times, it's catastrophic.

I hear myself moan as my body convulses into consciousness. That wasn't real? The dream—moments before, enjoyed in slumber—lingers about, fragmented. That actor from Facebook was onstage. He was dressed in the blue uniform of a security or corrections officer. The stage's wooden-planked floor was dusty from eons of neglect. Nobody came to the theater anymore. Lupita asked my opinion. He was beaming up there on stage, in between the thick curtains. We all applauded at the end of his performance. Fuck, how long have I been asleep?

Ten years . . . Cocaine.

Never is a long time.

I'm an addict. It's hard to convey what that truly means to someone who is not. Someone who is in control. Normal. Someone who doesn't lie in the dark staring at the shadows. Fantasizing guiltily about the last hit. The smell. The taste. The rush. The tingle starts in my upper shoulders. Moves down my spine and into my groin. I breathe out, and thankfully, I'm still in bed. This constant battle rages within me. *Never do drugs again.* That's what I promised myself. That's why I ran. I'm trying. I'm succeeding. For now. But never is a long time.

This is the end, my only friend. The end.

It hurts to set you free . . .

I'm ready. The rust is mostly gone. I feel like my old self again. Well, kind of. There's a lot of miles on this body; there's a lot of miles on this soul. My mind isn't as sharp as it once was, but I see the glimmer of the past me. I'm headed back.

A friend randomly sent me a text about starting over. He has no idea what I've been through or what I'm planning. The text contains the names of famous and rich Americans who started their businesses or careers later in life. Ray Kroc, Costco guy, some other dude. The names escape me, but the message does not. Now is my time. The first forty-two were . . . an adventure . . . and this next set won't be boring, but dammit, I'm going to focus. I'm not going to change so much as I'm going to be present. I won't float through pretending as if everyone else has power I do not.

Like, I can't change the fucking world. Because I can. Fuck this. These people aren't smarter than me. These people ain't better than me. These people are just more . . . *here* than me.

. . . But you'll never follow me

The end of laughter and soft lies . . .

Fuck. I can breathe again. I feel like smiling again. It's like this dark cloud of fear and depression and confusion is lifting, and I can see that little boy—standing there listening to his mother tell him that he can be president one day. I want to tell him to stand up and tell her to shut the fuck up. Bitch, no, I can't. Bitch, no I won't, and bitch, that's OK. I don't want to be president. I want to create—create images and sounds and dreams and destinies and money and love and power and children. I want to *be*. I don't want to click off notches on your status belt. I want to smell the crisp air and know that I am alive. I feel the shell of this past twenty-five years falling away. God, I can't believe how many times I thought of taking my life. Only responsibility and guilt kept me here. Sad. I didn't love myself enough. That's not noble, that's self-hate. Self-loathing. I'm scared, but motherfucker, I'm ready.

. . . The end of nights, we tried to die.

This is the end.

—Jim Morrison, The Doors

21

LOSING MY SHIT

W hy am I so nervous? I have been on a thousand auditions before. Gotta calm down, gotta relax. Must. Fucking. Breathe. OK, this is ridiculous. I can't do any worse than the time I went on an audition high. That was the worst idea—not just for the obvious reasons, but for the paranoia. I swore the casting people could tell I was high. Were they laughing at me? Did she see me dip into the bathroom? I tried to clean myself up before I went in, ran into a Duane Reade and bought nasal spray and gum. If you ever run into someone consuming large amounts of nasal spray and gum, they are high as fucking hell and desperate to come down. That was the dumbest shit ever. Should I have stayed home?

I went in anyway. You can't not show up for an audition. The worst thing you can do as an actor is not show up.

Casting directors are used to people sucking and even being late, but not showing up is a way to never be called again. Think about it: even if you're sick as shit, you may look like what they want. If you look like the character, they may find a way to use you anyway. Limit the lines. Allow you to have the script near you. I once had a director switch up an entire commercial because my costar couldn't read, but she was drop-dead gorgeous, and in the end, what's more important? So what? I had to find a way to discuss menstrual cramps from my point of view.

Cocaine makes my jaw go haywire; it moves involuntarily—not when you want it to at all. It's difficult to say lines when your jaw won't fucking work. It doesn't get that way right away either. It started to hit me in the waiting room. All the actors are chatting, and I'm chillin'. Some asshole decides to be a smart ass and ask me what time is my slot. My lips can't move. Fuck. Panic. Sweat. Lots of sweat. I bolt to the bathroom, and I'm dripping. This is not going well. I can't breathe, I can't talk, and I'm sweating like I just came out of the shower at LA Fitness (no ventilation in there, plus I'm nervous about the fungus, so it makes it worse).

Can't turn back now. My group gets called. Surprisingly, my audition goes much worse than I feared. Nose dripping, forehead sweating, jaw malfunctioning, plus the director asks me to pantomime flipping burgers with no props at all, accentuating the hand tremors I'm experiencing. My response? Finish my coke in the bathroom.

My point is . . . relax. You may fuck up today, but hey, at least you're not high on coke.

We all say we want to be famous and rich and rule the world. I am no different. But when I see them—the rich, the famous, the world leaders—I feel different. I don't feel like them. I don't look like them. I don't think like them. These fame whores pandering their souls for riches. Could I be one of them? Could I pimp myself, my family, my existence to reach the stratosphere? They are so fucking dumb. I can see it. Shit, when I'm with them, I can smell the stupidity. They wrap themselves in their money and Instagram philosophical motivations to inspire me to hustle. Prevent me from sleeping. Strip me of the habits that have prevented me from reaching their heights, but in actuality, that isn't how they got there. I know. I come from money. I have lived with these people. They are ignorant, stubborn, deceitful . . . and lucky, most of all.

They pretend to know something that we don't, but in the end, all they know is no shame.

Ha.

I'm one to talk. Presently sitting in an NYC cafe, downing old-fashioneds in a desperate attempt to cure my nerves. I can't go over this fucking script again. Cannot do it.

Phil, the security guard.

Fuck Phil. How did this come to pass? How did Phil

become a step up? Do they not know I'm the guy from the lottery commercial? Life is cruel. The things we want most require the talents we possess least.

I'm talented, smart, engaging, and caring.

But I'm not for sale.

So watch out, casting! I'm on my way. I'm tired. I have to take a shit. I'm drunk.

And I don't give a fuck if I book this shit.

Aside from the fact that I don't know what today is, it's all gravy.

Weren't we happier before Facebook? Before social media, people posting their rants, and philosophies, and ideologies on every platform they can find. Their opinions on the Oregon standoff and Black Lives Matter and the presidential debate. They post as if we care, as if they matter. They craft their clever words and press send with great personal satisfaction as their thoughts hurtle into the stratosphere. They mean nothing. To most of the world, they mean nothing. No, really. They mean absolutely nothing.

You may feel a lighter personal load, having unpackaged your thoughts. But it means nothing. What is the point? To profess enough wisdom to garner attention as a political commentator? Do you think that CNN or the Rainbow Coalition or the *New York Times* is going to pick up on your string of posts and demand that you immediately report to their local bureau to be hired as a correspondent? It's not going to happen.

Even worse are the bastards telling us about how great their lives are. Do I need to know where you are going on vacation? Is this for me to feel happy for you, or disgust in my lack of adventure and mobility? Wonderful for you that your new car has finally arrived to transport your newborn child to his private school graduation/sports banquet/recruiting session. Tell us how the new corporation you and your partners are forming is going to make shitloads of money, changing the world as you dine with your perfectly angled wife at a four-star restaurant.

We are in love with ourselves. Strike that—we are in love with our online selves. Spending way too much time crafting this persona we dream of being. In reality, we hate ourselves. We are reminded every day we log on how much we haven't accomplished, how that girl/guy got away, and how broke we are. For what? Because we all want to be famous. We want to matter. Social media has fooled us into believing we do. It's like drugs. Drugs short-circuit the dopamine system. They allow you to feel joy without actually doing anything. The same goes for social media. It allows you to feel important without actually being important. And just like drugs, it short-circuits the system until one day you look up and you have 6,000 selfies (of 8,790 total) posted on Instagram for your 328 followers. So post your duck-lipped, cayenne pepper–challenged, duct-taping dietary triumph breakup advice call to revolution.

You aren't important.

You aren't famous.

You are insane.

Shoulda, coulda, woulda.

A dear friend of mine has a tattoo that reads NO REGRETS. It is emblazoned across his wrist. I am not certain if it is a permanent testament to the way he has lived his life or an impetus for how he should view it. Or really what the difference is. Bottom line is that could never be me or never be on me. I am full of regrets. Full of "what if?" "I should have done that," and "wish I said this."

I regret meeting Colin. To the world, he is an aging artist, dying of kidney failure. To me, he is a vampire . . . *my* vampire. He bit me and killed me and then let me drink his blood. The beginning was exhilarating. It was full of energy and magic and promise and mystery. But just like in the movies, it didn't last. The good times gave way to the truth about addiction. It now envelopes my entire life; my every move and decision is either a step away or a step toward.

I regret not attending law school. I suppose I could enroll at Temple and grind it out. It's never too late. I would be showing my children a great example—not just talking about it, but really being about it. My senior yearbook plans were to attain my law degree and be a sports agent. How happy would I be if I had stuck to my plan? Instead, I majored in TV production. I followed my friends to Howard and studied TV production. I turned down scholarships from Lehigh, Brown, and Catholic University to attend Howard University on an Annenberg Scholarship. A scholarship I was awarded after writing one paper. One. Paper.

I regret hurting all those women, jumping from bed to bed. Maybe it's because I have a daughter now and see how emotionally unstable women are from a different perspective. Maybe I see how woefully unequipped I am to help her with her future heartbreak. I regret what I did and who I did it to. I wish I had been stronger. Better. More mature.

These mistakes, though. These flaws. They are what make me, and it wasn't all bad. I met my wife through these flaws. I gained an insight into the world that nobody else can share. I have a story to tell. I have knowledge to share. I am not sure if I have NO REGRETS, but fuck it. I ain't looking back.

And isn't that divine?

Romany Malco said, "People want affirmation, not information." So true. White privilege isn't something we can define; it is something that exists. It is something that just is. This thing permeates our society. It's woven into the fabric of our being. I live in an all-white neighborhood—well, majority white. There is the two-block stretch of homes on Spring Street occupied by a majority of black people and the core of our state championship basketball streak. Other than that, it's white and Jewish and me.

My friends come from all walks of life. I seamlessly move from group to group, regardless of race, creed, socioeconomics, or political ideology. My ex-wife has often asked me how I do that. I respond that I strive to be interested, not interesting; therefore, there is no pressure on me to be anything but a good listener.

My background is portrayed as an anomaly in America. According to the media, the majority of blacks live in poverty. The true number is 30 percent. Now, when compared with whites at 10 percent, it is striking. But even more so is the weight we give the 30 percent. That segment of our population dominates the 70 percent. It dominates when I turn on my television and am bombarded by tales from the 30—whether it be crime reporting or stories of triumph, it's the 30. Fiction to nonfiction, it's the 30. Music, fashion, and culture is the 30. We are saturated by this "fact" that blacks are all in this continuous struggle for survival, and many of us are. It jades all our thinking. I grew up thinking of myself as this lone beacon of black middle class-dom, even though I grew up across the street from a real-life version of *The Cosby Show*. Television was more real. Athletes seem to all rise from the ranks of poverty. We are told that our way out of the ghetto is through athletic prowess, yet 70 percent of us don't live in the ghetto, and most of the 70 didn't do it by playing sports.

When looking for the number of black doctors, I am struck by the sheer volume of articles dedicated to the dwindling numbers. However, what I saw was that in 1968, there were, like, two thousand black doctors. Today, there are close to twenty thousand. According to stats, these numbers have been dwindling. However, there are no articles bemoaning the fact that there are only 446 NBA players. Four hundred and forty six. And not all of them are black. For some reason, these success stories receive far more attention than what is the everyday, humdrum route to success. Somehow, the rise of former drug dealers to millionaire rappers is what is force-fed to us. The swagger, the lingo, the culture is all heaped upon us. We are all the same ... but we are not.

White privilege isn't something I can simplify; it is very complicated. White privilege means never having to explain to your son how to come home alive, never having to explain to your daughter how to tell her friends not to brush her hair. Never having to listen to your white friends "revoke" your street cred when they see where you grew up. Never having to worry about being maced by a single female in a dark parking lot. Never being pulled over and asked what you are doing here. Never having to remind yourself that despite what the media is telling you, 70 percent of people who look like you are doing well and succeeding and achieving.

My family belongs to a group called Jack and Jill. It is a social group for black mothers and children. Whenever a perspective family asks me why I want my kids in Jack and

Jill, I answer the same exact way: I don't want my kids to think that I am the only black man with a black wife who has his own business and can speak properly. In fact, I want my kids to see that people who look like them are researchers, professors, lawyers, doctors, developers, engineers, designers ...

White privilege is always knowing who you are and never having to explain what that is.

22

LOSING MY SHIT...AGAIN

No, Kyle, I don't care what Bun B or anybody else thinks about Rick Ross. I recline into my chair, sipping a peach vodka–infused Arnold Palmer. Kyle's blabbering is becoming increasingly aggressive. The sweat beads on his forehead are multiplying. I'm not certain whether the impetus is his inner rage or the chemicals he used to process his hair into that Jodeci-esque curl. It's taking me a great deal more energy to hide my disdain for his idiocy than it does to counter his arguments. The ladies in the room are trying to be polite. They try to change the subject. Maybe they fear this conversation will turn violent, and they all know I would probably lose that exchange as handily as I am winning the current verbal one.

No, Kyle, I don't care if you have convened among the wise men of hip-hop, sat among the gods of rap, and observed their reaction to Rick's entrance. I'm not saying you are lying. Maybe you were there. Maybe you are always there. Your stories certainly seem plausible. They are rife with the normal details of guns, drugs, profanity, and sex. I just don't care. OK, so they don't respect Rick Ross—or, as you tragically continue to refer to him, "Officer Ricky." I have a little news flash for you, Kyle: I don't respect them or their opinions.

Why does it matter? Why does Rick Ross have to be telling the truth for me to enjoy his music? Why is hip-hop so obsessed with "realism"? Why hasn't it been allowed to evolve beyond that? I get it. It's supposed to be the "CNN of the streets," but do the reporters have to create the news as well as report it? When I sit down in a theater and watch Will Smith save the world or Christian Bale fight evil computers, I don't expect them to be those characters off screen. So Rick Ross probably didn't fly birds across the Atlantic in his business dealing with Manuel Noriega . . . so fucking what? As a matter of fact, I don't want him to. He would probably be getting arrested and incarcerated, and then he wouldn't be able to make any more music. It's unfortunate that this music that can so thoroughly represent us is instead impeded by our ignorance and rigidity.

So you can narrow your eyes and raise your voice and laugh condescendingly all night long. When it comes to my music, I prefer the ability to produce art over the accounting of your past existence.

And that's a Jheri curl, asshole.

I didn't say that, of course. Dude is a guest in my home, brother of my good friend the Diggy Diggy Doc. I will sit and continue to suffer through this barrage of gangster idiocy. Kyle is incredulous at my defiance in the face of the prevailing hip-hop sentiment. Doc pours him another white wine. Irony. He continues with his lesson in "real hip-hop" from the days of yore. Before skinny jeans and auto-tune, a time when designer clothes were mispronounced with an attitude and knocked off with pride. The Golden Age of Hip-Hop, and to some extent I agree with him. The eighties and nineties featured some great artists.

I discovered rap with Tom McGill at the time I was attending Walnut Crest Academy and had fully assimilated into their (white) culture. I'm not sure *assimilate* is a strong enough word, to be honest. I wanted to be white. I would stare at myself in the mirror and wish to be light skinned. On several shopping trips to the department store, I would lag behind in the makeup aisle, pretending to be in protest of my mother's activity choice for our Saturday afternoon. Secretly, I was taking stock of all the different products, trying to identify the right cream to turn me into that epitome of perfection. The white man. My mother was absolutely responsible for this. We can debate whether other hang-ups and bullshit rattling around in my head are a result of her or me or outside sources . . . but self-hate? That's all you, Mom.

From a young age, she would relax my hair. *Relax my hair*. The lathered goop was slopped all over my follicles while the edges of my skin were protected with Vaseline. We would wait however many minutes, and then the burning would start. It would begin slowly, then *ouch!* That shit hurt like a motherfucker. I wore a bandana at night to try to lay my hair down, and as I slept, I dreamed of marrying a white woman to have biracial kids (because we all know they make the prettiest babies).

Sidebar: that shit is weird: how two butt-ugly people from different races can create the most beautiful children. I ran into a friend from my high school days at the park. Jeff (I forget his last name) introduced me to his wife and child. Now, I'm not gonna say Jeff is ugly, but we did call him "George Jefferson" in high school. And now, instead of cutting off that offensive hairline with the vast region of baldness in the back, this fool outlined it. His wife, though . . . oh, she was ugly as shit and fat and white.

Damn, that baby was cute.

Anyway, the point is I really hated myself, and I was drawn to white culture. I loved Metallica, Anthrax, the Sex Pistols, et cetera. Then one day over at Tom's house, he popped in a tape of this band he was about to go see at Franklin Field. We were sitting in his basement looking at magazines. The homogeneous rolls of sleeping bags and sheets were indistinguishable from each other. I was half-asleep because we had stayed up all night watching movies.

He asked me if I had heard this new shit; the name didn't even pique my interest. Then he pressed play, and my whole world changed. "Rock Box" by Run-DMC screamed out the speakers. Maybe it was the perfect combination of rock and hip-hop that grabbed me. Certainly, I had heard other rap before, but this was different, and it made me analyze everything I had heard before . . . or since. The guitar riffs and the leather jackets and pants and the fedoras . . . These guys were cool, yet different . . . like how I wanted to be. They made me reexamine my perception of myself. I began to look at the history of music and found at its core (at least here in the United States) black musicians, and our culture had been appropriated time and time again. In my house, Elvis had been king, but now I knew him to be a mere pretender to the throne. Just another puppet paraded out by the machine to transform our "dangerous" ghetto, gutter discord into something safe for white America to consume.

Yes, this was music. And I loved it. I began to speak in rap lyrics in casual conversation. I didn't do it out of affectation; I sincerely thought in terms of their lyrics. They were poets. They were my scribes. My inspiration. Their words spoke to me and for me. Even though their experiences were a world away, they might as well have been living on the moon. But the way they were able to convey that world separated them from any world.

So here I sit, patiently waiting my turn to speak in my own home. Kyle spits venomously toward me. The words don't even matter to me anymore. He has decided to ignore their art. It is convenient; it is easy to do. Unfortunately, they themselves feel the need to perpetuate this obvious contrast. The money. It's the money. It does them all in. Millions of dollars to speak your mind, to make up stories, and all you have to do is pretend it's all true. No. It doesn't make sense. Stephen King doesn't kill people. J. K. Rowling isn't a witch. We accept this. We consume these things right alongside our music. Anita Baker didn't have to have her heart broken, and New Edition didn't really have to call the "telephone man." For some reason, however, the fact that William Roberts, a.k.a. Rick Ross, probably never manufactured or distributed huge amounts of cocaine throughout the United States is a problem. Shit. To me, that's his genius: his ability to watch, listen, learn, and turn around and create music that not only encapsulates perfectly what that life is all about, but inspires us as it entertains. That's art. But Kyle doesn't care. For some reason, he thinks the fact that Bun B or Lil Wayne and them sneered at Ross in his presence should validate all he is saying. Sad. Fuck them. Fuck them for trying to dupe us. Rick is better than they are. There, I said it. In effect, all they did was tell you what they saw. Can't anybody do that? Rick has an imagination. He created himself in the image he wanted to be.

And he won.

So I look down at my bamboo floors as Kyle's words spatter about. I see the pain in everyone's eyes as they bore of our conversation. Migos's "Pipe It Up" is blaring from my surround sound, and I am happy.

Happy because the veins in my forehead aren't bursting like Kyle's. Happy that I haven't limited my musical experiences based on arbitrary parameters. Happy that Rick Ross is rich while Bun B is famous. Happy that thirty-two years later, I still love music. All music. White music, black music, old music, and new music. Just happy. A smile creeps on my face. Kyle sees I am unwavering. He drinks more of my white wine. I tell him to never stop listening to new music; it makes you grow old. He'd rather be old.

Maybe I'm just happy I'm not Kyle.

23

COUP DE GRACE

They say everything happens for a reason . . . whenever they don't know the reason. When something catastrophic has occurred, and everyone is just standing there staring in slack-jawed consternation, it's human nature to pretend that what they have witnessed makes sense. Perfect sense, I guess.

Today didn't seem any different. Here I go once again, waking up to somebody else's life. My family whirring about in the morning. The kids and the wife and the dog and the cat and the breakfast and the school bus and the shouting and the arguing and the compromising. My familiar chaos. Nothing different.

No, no. Wait! It's totally different. No chaos. No family. No . . . nothing. The wife and the kids left, remember?

Guilty relief. I am left to fend for myself. I have every intention of doing so.

This morning's shower doesn't feel so . . . desperate. It doesn't feel like cult water baptizing me. I don't feel any . . . pressure. Is it because they are so far away? Today I can be anything I want to be. I don't have to pretend to go to work and sit in the Starbucks and stare at people and pine away for that creative spark they must have felt that propelled them to sit there and write that manuscript/novel/poem/song.

I can have whatever I want for breakfast. Whatever I want to drink. Seven a.m. cocktail? You betcha! I settle for a joint I rolled in reserve from a dime bag I bought from some little kid on the street. I support small businesses. Young entrepreneurs. I inhale. Tastes funny, but fuck it. It's all going great. I even halfway start feeling like I actually want to go to work. Maybe I can actually accomplish something today. Maybe I just have too much responsibility on my hands. Family and business? I need to slack on one, right? I should have put more work into my business systems. Just then my phone rings on the kitchen counter, and it's my assistant from work. DPW is back with the health department. They are looking for blood. My chest starts to tighten. I know I said something to get off the phone. I'm not sure what. What can you say? "Fuck it, I want them to close me down anyway?" I hang up the phone, and when I look up, I see tears in my eyes. My nose is running. Wait, what?

And that's when the voices started.

They are a low murmur at first, like conga drums in the distance. I can't quite make out what they are trying to say. One voice breaks through the homogeneity and blares like an alto sax. The staccato rhythm is deafening at this point. Another voice bangs in my head like Animal and his drums from the Muppets. OK, I am going fuckin' crazy. I'm looking around, and I clearly see no one here. I gotta get some help. That pot was laced. Little bastard. So of course, I call my drug dealer.

Ghafar's number is so familiar; I've erased it a thousand times, but I can recall it by heart. In my dreams, in my nightmares, gun to my head, running through a field of daisies, I can remember Ghafar. He meets me right at my front door. Delivery! We exchange pleasantries, money, and cocaine. That first sniff felt so good. It always did. It always does. I let it sink in. Deep. In. Then more cocaine. Eyes blurred, world disappearing. I'm floating away from here. That joint is a distant memory.

The voices dissipate. No more jazz in my head. It's not peaceful, though. No, not by any stretch of the imagination. The hallucinations come murky and obscure. The paranoia is dark and sudden. It's under my skin. In my head. I can see the cameras staring in my windows. I can see them.

I'm crawling on the floor trying not to be seen by the cameras and telescopes staring from my neighbors' houses. I must close the shades so they can't see me. I'm sweating, and my clothes are getting dirty. Did I just hear something in the basement? I grab a knife from the kitchen and investigate. There are too many shadow people running around down here. It's frightening. I stab at the air in the dark corners of the basement. I hear them laughing upstairs. I run upstairs. They are too fucking quick. So fucking quick.

I call my wife for help. She answers, but I can "hear" she has company. Not just company; I can "hear" she is having sex with someone. She can't even stop having sex long enough to answer the phone? I'm yelling at her. She's crying. She doesn't understand what I am talking about. Why am I saying these things? What's going on? I hang up the phone and peek out the window. I can "see" her car in the neighbor's driveway. I'm sweating and running to get dressed. I'm going to catch her!

I'm outside, wild coke eyes scanning for signs of her. Where is she? Succubus evil witch! Where? Damn, I took too long getting dressed. She escaped. Wait! Did I just see her car turn the corner? The corner comes into focus on my approach. I must catch her. She is probably going to the airport. Uber! I call for an Uber to pick me up. Two minutes to pickup. Great fuckin' app. I should invent an app. I should invent something. More cocaine should help with that. *Sniiiiiff.* Ahh!

The Uber driver is telling me something. I can't hear what he is saying. I can't hear what the voices are saying. I can't hear what I am saying. Did he just say the app is now down, and I have to pay cash? That's impossible. I just used the app, and I only have two hundred-dollar Johns. Did he just say he is going to rob and murder me? Oh no, he is not. Not today, buddy. I'm out. Of the car. Out.

I'm jumping out of a moving car. I hit the road like a stuntman, rolling and popping up to sprint in the opposite direction. My mouth tastes like blood and gravel. My head hurts. My heart is pounding in my throat. Sweat blinding me. Or is it tears? Uber comes to a screeching halt, but he won't be able to make a U-turn here. Joke's on you and your shadow men! You will never catch me. Never! Turn down this alley. A dead end. A twenty-foot fence. No problem. Up and over. Can't stop. Can't let them catch me. Shadow men everywhere. Running alongside me. Parallel streets, parallel world. Can't run anymore, can't find my way. Crashing. Down. Head. Spinning. People over me. Cell phones out. What happened to us? Empathy has given way to videography. I'm very tired. I cannot stand. These aren't shadow men helping me up. I feel them. I see them. I smell them. No life in their eyes, but they are real people. But they are cop people leading me to the cop van. I curl up on the floor. Crying. Ah, so that's why people revert to the fetal position. It feels like comfort. Safe. Mommy. Home. I just want to sleep.

And so I do.

That's me in the corner, smoking a cigarette by myself. Mostly everyone here is mentally alone, but I choose to physically separate as well. I don't want to be like them. I don't think I am like them. I have cared for them for most of my life, and I thought I understood them. Thought I was better than them. But here I stand . . . one of them?

"Drug-induced psychosis from cocaine toxicity" is the diagnosis I am given. The doctors here say I should count my lucky stars that I am still alive. You see, overdosing is always the acute amount of a drug you take. Sometimes it's the amount of the shit you sniffed—all built up in your blood and organs—and that last bump/line/puff puts you over the threshold. I went over the threshold. I went way over the line. I didn't die, but my brain was fucked. You don't ever fully recover from that kind of scrambling. So yeah, here I am sitting in a crisis response center. It's where they send you when you are acting like a complete maniac in the middle of the street. Shitting your pants, screaming at cars, pushing a cart full of clothes, naked against traffic, or just doing your best to avoid shadow men. Welcome home. For at least forty-eight hours.

Code 302. That's an involuntary commitment for mental health reasons. They can only keep you for forty-eight hours against your will. After that, they have to bring you into mental health court, where a petitioner will explain to the magistrate why you are bat-shit crazy and have to stay inside.

How many times have I showed up to court? Ten? Fifteen? Twenty? Sat in that waiting room listening to the insane on the other side of the wall. Their mental torment too much for them to conceal, even with the chance of freedom dangled before them. Too much torture. I see them from the inside out now. I think about how many times I heard my name called as a petitioner. Walked into that magistrate's room, placed my hand on that Bible, and swore to tell the truth. Swore. Then proceeded to lie. Not huge lies, yet lies nonetheless. Necessary exaggerations. I had to. I swear. They needed more than forty-eight hours, man. They needed forty-eight years. They needed evaluation and contemplation and much more than I could ever give them at home. So I said they were violent and non-compliant and a danger to themselves and others. Whatever I needed to.

Listen, they didn't even know what was happening: sitting there talking to the voices and screaming and cursing and threatening and "crazy-ing"! Meanwhile, I just signed their asses up for another lifetime of "help."

I wondered who might show up for my court date. My wife? My mom and dad? The police?

That's the orderly coming for me now. His eyes stare blankly, disconnected from this reality just as much as the rest of us. His brain focused on Instagram posts, weekly paychecks, and quitting time. Not too much different. We wade through the insane toward the door that leads to free-dom. All last night, I lay awake, excited to get the hell out of here, but as we get closer, my heart starts to pound in my chest, and my throat tightens. It's starting to dawn on me how much I may need to stay. Look at them. Look at us.

I mean, they can say it was the cocaine, but really, it was "crazy" dusted in white powder, snorted through a rolled-up dollar earned from the crazy.

It happened. It was real. I lost my mind. I have been losing it for quite some time, honestly. Dealing with the responsibility of human lives and fighting the government and staff and subcontractors and inspectors and taxes has been tearing me apart. Frayed at the ends. No way to deny it. Look at me. Addict. Psychotic. Inpatient. Look at me. I can't leave. I know better! I know what I am, and I know where this leads and how it ends. That's what everyone does— demands freedom over health. Independence over inner peace. Well, I can't.

The lights inside here are fluorescent. Hot. They buzz. Everyone knows that they do. I mean, everyone is familiar with the buzz. The *hum*, if you will. But when you are here —really here, not-going-home-anytime-soon "here"—it's louder. More forceful. Penetrating. Annoying. It creates a filter too. It's like living in an Instagram post. All fuzzy and vibrant. No pores. I try to relax. I need to relax. Scanning the scene, trying my best to blend my black body into these white, white walls. I see but do not want to be seen. Look at them. Crazy as hell. Maybe science has gone too far. Maybe we don't need to cure *every* disease. Thin the herd.

Shit. Is she coming right for me? Oh God. I can't back up any farther. The wall is too hard. Her mouth is crusty and chapped, and her hair is greasy. I am sure she normally dresses in shit-covered layers, but thankfully, we all have robes on. Yeah, my name is Earl. Yeah, I stay on this floor. Well, kind of. I mean, I don't stay. I mean, I won't stay for long. What the fuck does she want? Is she trying to hold a conversation with me? *Me?* I am not like her. Like . . . them. I'm different, goddammit! She has a point, though. The food does suck. I never paid attention to the monotony of food before, but she has a point. Applesauce, grilled cheese, and juice are getting a little fucking old. I'm an adult, for God's sake.

Her name is Priscilla. She has been repeatedly raped by her father for ten years. Finally, she broke. Her mind broke. She has a twitch with her head when she speaks and a click in her jaw. She confides in me. Unwanted confession. She liked it at first. Thought it meant that her father loved her. Birthdays, holidays, and trips. Then anytime he wanted. Conflicted. Confused. Her mind just broke one day. And so she is here with the crazies. She is crazy. Talking to me about culinary choices or rather the lack thereof. I can't concentrate. I'm too angry. Yes, angry. How the fuck does she not realize I am not one of them? I'm not like her. I'm a fucking sane person. I run these kinds of places. I admit people like you and place you in beds and monitor your medications and hygiene and comings and goings. There's no *we*. Understand? *We* aren't doing shit. *We* aren't experiencing shit. *We* aren't going to ask for anything. I'm just taking a break real quick. A respite. Right? We aren't the fucking same!

Oh shit. My head starts to swim a bit, and my chest is getting tight again. If I have a panic attack in here, they will never let me out. The meds are mild, and she is pushing me over their limitations. Go away! Priscilla smiles, and her rotten teeth reflect the lights. No filter for those. Revolting. "Get away from me, bitch," I want to yell at her. I want to strangle her. I am not like her. Stop talking to me. Stop! This situation is unacceptable. A crazy talking to me like I am her fucking peer. Crazy. I am not one of them. Am I?

I've been caring for other people for so long, I gotta be selfish and take care of myself.

So I stayed. In the crazy house. With my people. Our people.

* * *

My ex-wife and I drove home in the rain. In the silence. She tried to talk to me about what had happened, but her tears and sobbing were just too much. Unable to comfort her and explain, I stared out the window as she drove. Philadelphia sped by in gray and dark highlights. The SEPTA buses splashed pedestrians draped in glistening capes. Faceless. No matter how hard it rained, the city still looked dirty to me. Corner stores and trash and cars and zombies.

My life had been spent here, and I didn't know what happened to either. She hadn't told my kids or anyone else where I was or what had happened. Told everyone I was in Vegas celebrating a friend's birthday. It's good to be the boss, right? I can be anywhere I want. Even when I'm not there.

I pushed past the kids. Barely hugged them. Couldn't look them in the face. Too ashamed. Too weak. Not worthy. Please don't be like me, guys. Grow up strong and smart and talented and contribute to society. Not like me. The bed felt wonderful. I slept. When I awoke, the house was empty. She made breakfast and left it on the stove. While I ate, I tried to imagine a normal day. Knew I had to go into the office. Breathe in deeply. Suck it up. This thing that brings me life, pays our Johns, provides my everything is killing me at the same damn time. It's fucked up. I have been caring for them so long that now I'm turning into them. Maybe always have been one of them. One of "us." So what should I do? Quit?

The door opened to Argyle Street . . . that old carcass of a building. It all . . . seemed . . . normal. Nobody knew. They just asked me the same bullshit, mind-numbing questions as usual. This was broken; that person's missing; who just died; we need to replace this and repair that. Normal. Ah, but here comes Nancy. Clown shoes shuffling. Clothes too big. A moving mountain of laundry with bags and bags of food, clothing, and supplies "t-o-o." Here she comes. Shuffles right up to me and smiles. That knowing Nancy smile.

Those eyes smile at me as well. She gets a little closer. Closer than I let my clients normally get. Baring her brown teeth smiling, she giggles, then simply says, "Enjoy the ride?"

24

THEN WHY

Why? I can't remember why. I'm sitting here desperately scanning the nether regions of my cortex. Recalling some awful story. Feeling. Something. Give me the why. But nothing. Nothing comes. It has been too long. Is that something that happens? Do all addicts sit at some point and ask why? Is this simply a part of the process?

I haven't touched anything since . . . damn, I can't remember. I should be happy. Zero slipups. No temptations. This should be a celebration of will, a testament to the new me, but instead, here I am, awake at four o'clock in the morning, wondering . . . why?

It makes me nervous, this wondering. My leg is jumping up and down. Thankfully, I'm three thousand miles away from my drug dealer, yet my mind is beginning to think.

Beginning to work the angles. The wheels are turning. I feel them. I had already turned down several opportunities to return home for business because I knew I wasn't ready. I turned them down because I knew what I would do when that plane touched down. The number, though erased from my phone and pushed to the outer region of my memory, would flood back to me. A tide of despair gently crashing into the shore. Slowly eroding my resolve. "I don't like cocaine; I just enjoy the smell."

I have no idea what I'm doing here. Literally, no idea. The world is a confusing and large and scary place. Should I stay in my safe zone in Philadelphia? Maybe I should just travel more or take up golf and swing by my neighbors' barbeques, but I'm not happy. Not fulfilled. Maybe those ambitions aren't worthy. Maybe contentment comes before enjoyment, but I will never know. I need to jump. Run. Break the loop. The television series *Westworld* has been fascinating me. I am not the only one. I feel this eerie connection to the hosts. The robots. They live their lives on a looped narrative. A tech erases the rapes and murders and deaths they experience, only so that they may merrily experience them the next day. Some of the hosts begin to have "memories." They begin to remember another life, another death. I feel like them. Felt like them . . . feel like them? I have to move. The loop has gotten dangerous. The drugs and the depression and the drinking. They're out of hand, and increasing the toxicity of the situation is my uncanny ability to hide it all from everyone. Or am I? Maybe that was my loop. That I thought nobody noticed. That I was getting away with it.

Wasn't it my imagination? Sitting in that state inspection, unable to breathe. Those two motherfuckers sitting across the table from me, yammering away about nothing. Nothing I cared about, at least. Rifling through my files, telling me what an awful job I was doing, accusing me of stealing and not caring for my clients. Forget about the fact I'm getting pennies a day to care for these people. Thirty-four bucks a day, goddammit! So what if I didn't sign the back of the fourth page of the annual screening for my client who has lived here for four years? I think I know the fucking client. Obviously, I approve of them being here. Can't I just sign it now? What the fuck? Aren't we on the same team? Don't we just want the best for these poor forgotten fucks? Or are you just interested in busting my fucking balls? Huh? Huh?

And look at me, pretending I had allergies or a cold. Excusing myself to sniff glorious cocaine in the bathroom. Maybe it was my imagination—my imagination that I got away with it. That nobody noticed. Nobody's the wiser. But maybe when I went to the bathroom, they looked at each other and sighed. Shook their heads, lamented a life lost. Meanwhile, I stared wide eyed and sleep deprived into a smeared mirror in my dungeon-office basement . . . maybe.

I'm sitting here at five o'clock in the morning, asking myself what I'm doing here. But honestly, what was I doing there? Everyone else seems to have it all figured out. I can't seem to concentrate. Maybe it was Craig. Was he the last straw?

Craig Kelly. Fifty-something-year-old nothing. Life over . . . before it really began. Cannot remember how he got here, but he got here, and here he was. Brown skin, sad eyes, and a fixation for fashion, albeit picked from your local dumpster. His daily accoutrements were impressive: shined shoes, pressed trousers, button-down shirt and vest. His daily adventures were none of my concern. His nightly dalliances weren't either. The trash he picked began to pile up, however, and this became a problem.

That's me in the back of Argyle Street, standing next to an inspector, trying to look sober while discussing the mountain of trash that has accumulated. The city won't give me a dumpster permit, and my rear neighbor won't grant me access for private hauling, so I have been carrying trash in the back of my Chevy Avalanche to the dump weekly. Weekly, I haul thirty bags of garbage to the dump. Weekly, I stand in the back of my $50,000 Avalanche pickup with the roaches, bedbugs, and mice, tossing contractor-size bags into a trash truck while the obese dispatcher/operator leans on his cane, watching and smirking.

Does he know I have a college degree? Maybe he knows I have a drug habit. Maybe he is just an asshole. I know I am.

Craig is adding to the pile. He is a dumpster diver, selling his wares on the street and in our home. The old radios and VHS players and books and necklaces and TVs and suitcases full of little girls' clothes are piling up. I can't take it anymore. Craig and I need to have a talk. Coincidentally, he believes the same thing. His demeanor is different today. The swagger he normally exudes has eroded. Maybe his cocaine habit is catching up with him. I know mine is killing me. He looks terrible. We look terrible. Lucky bastard can go to meetings. Where can I go? I can't just show up in a church basement. And stand. And confess. What if Craig was there?

Craig needs me. Well, he needs my money. Bad. He is in debt to his drug dealer. I shouldn't have given him shit, but I did. Big heart. He paid me back. Then he paid me back again. The third time, he asked if I had enough. He was still piling shit up, and I was getting fed up, and it had to stop, and this time he asked for the money advance, and I said no. No, Craig, I am not a personal savings and loan. Not a bank, not your daddy, not your brother. No. As a matter of fact, you need to go clean up this shit in this room and out back. It's attracting roaches . . .

and . . .

and . . .

and . . .

Just go!

Then he called. No, not Craig. His drug dealer. The same as mine. Oh shit.

He had Craig and wanted a ransom. Three hundred dollars or "You'll never see him again," he tells me. Like, never, ever see him again? Like, "he never darkens your doorstep or dives into your trash cans again because he is working off his debt to me, the drug dealer" again, or does he mean "dropping his corpse off at the morgue or your front steps" never see him again? I know this guy. He is my dealer too. One of them. Or at least he was. He wasn't a killer, but I wasn't going to push him. God forbid he put a bullet in Craig's temple, and I have to explain to people how this murderous drug dealer got my number. How Craig does drugs all the time in my facility. God forbid.

I find myself driving aimlessly, thinking. The radio plays, and the sky darkens. "Dead," I say to myself. He would be better off dead. We all would. All of us addicts. Death would free him from this bondage. This enormous burden that life has become. The increasingly daunting speculation of continued life would cease. He would be at peace. I would envy him. Dead. It would be quick. Painless. Dead. I'm sitting in front of the ATM, contemplating his escape. Contemplating mine as well. Three hundred bucks or dead. Three hundred bucks or freedom. Three hundred bucks sounds cheap, honestly.

I pussy out and pay. Sorry, Craig. I know somewhere deep inside, you hoped the phone wouldn't ring. You hoped

I wouldn't come through with that cash. Next time, I won't. Don't even bother to call me, guys. I told them that. But this time, I came through, and Craig, you came home. Depressed. Back to Argyle Street. Back to your "life." You barely said thanks, but I understand. You couldn't do it yourself, and I wouldn't help you. So now you're not free.

You're not . . . dead.

25

POSTMORTEM

That's me crying in an airport stall. Again. Leaving my childhood home of forty-two years. Finally. Free? The weight of my decision pressed down on me as I stood in the security checkpoint line. I made it through. But almost lost it when that pesky TSA worker asked me to remove my shades for recognition. Verification. Like she's a facial recognition expert. I am me. Right? My bag scanned through. My body scanned through. I disrobed and redressed, and the world whirled around me. Thousands of passengers, all going somewhere. This time, I was as well. Going somewhere. The TV blared political discord. I was numb to it all. We all were. Are. Maybe today was the day we all died. Today the bomb dropped, and nuclear disaster was headed our way. None of us would have noticed. Too many necks craning downward, engaging carefully designed apps of distraction. I think.

A one-way ticket. Los Angeles. The entirety of my life, I have been searching for something. Searching. For something. Trying to discover what I was fighting. What was I running from? What was I afraid of? All this time, it was just me. You can't change you. You can change your surroundings. Mask yourself in alternative realities and material possessions and social media postings and motivational sayings and religious dogma, but look closely. Closely. And there you are. Standing in an airport not sure if you can move forward. Legs cemented firmly in place. Scared to continue on. Afraid to go back. This is life. A constant examination of choices. Crossroads. So I dip into this bathroom to hide. To think. To breathe. And to cry.

Think about all I have done. And all I have not. My past rushes clearly into view. It grabs me. I'm ashamed. The life I led wasn't worthy of me. My potential. My beginning. I wasted so much time, I'm afraid it may be too late. This movement may be too late. Too little. Too late.

I'm sitting in the stall, tears streaming down from my eyes. I'm leaving. Leaving them. My people. My residents. My family. I don't want to. I finally understand them. I truly love them. I respect them. I am them, though they are stronger than me. If I had stayed, I would have crumbled. Fallen apart. So I am going. With some help, I got sober. With some meds, I got sane. And so I am running away from home. Running away from all that I know. Ashamed that I am not strong enough to stay. Ashamed they helped me more than I helped them. Afraid of what may lie ahead. Afraid of what I have left behind.

I'm wiping my eyes in the stall. Thinking about all of them. Twenty years of them. In and out of my facility. My life. So many stories. So many lives. I want to call them all and tell them thanks. Apologize for what I couldn't do right.

Instead, I reach into my pocket and pull out some Trident gum. The orange pack. Rehab must be working. I stand up straight and look at me in the mirror. It feels like I have never seen myself before. There I am. I have a life to lead. I have a family to reunite. This life is a gift. I have to be strong. Be thankful. I'm ready.

That's me getting on the plane. Easing down the jetway and into my seat. Staring out the window while strangers pretend to be interested in my life but secretly are deathly afraid of silence. I talk to them, but I don't know what I am saying. It doesn't matter. The stewardess is serving me snacks, and I am wondering what my life will become. Breathe deep. Focus. Sleep. I watch a documentary on low-income housing, and the thought of sixty-three thousand homeless children forms a lump in my throat. I cannot fix every problem in this world. We cannot save all of us. We don't have to. I get it now. But we can save ourselves. Fix our houses. Fix our minds. Face this life without fear and do our best to live our best. Twenty years I sat at that desk, wasting away. Twenty fucking years. My partner wants me to make a film with him, and my wife is open to taking me back. Sober and sane. Good things.

I have to be honest, I don't know exactly what I am going to do next, but I won't sit still.

Waiting to die.

ACKNOWLEDGMENTS

Thank you to my amazing mother and father. As a child, I could not fully understand all that you were doing for me. I could not understand what you were trying to instill in me. As an adult, I am not sure I could ever truly thank you for the sacrifices, the love, and the counsel you have given me. I would say that you have made me the man I am today, but I am not sure that that measures up.

Adrienne, Zoie, and Zakhari, you guys are my inspiration. All I have ever wanted was to leave something behind for you guys. All I ever wanted was to inspire you to be passionate about life and make you proud. (Maybe I will accomplish that in the next book LOL.) I love you guys more than life itself!

To everybody at Kingston Imperial, but especially Marvis Johnson, thank you for taking a chance on me.

Thank you for making a dream come true. I still cannot believe this is happening.

Thank you to Kathy Iandoli for taking a young writer under your wing. This would not exist if not for you. To my friends Jordan and Kamau, who were brave enough to read this and provide honest and sometimes harsh feedback, I thank you so much. To my staff and residents, I am inspired by your dedication and perseverance. And finally, this book is dedicated to my client of twenty years whom we lost during the pandemic, Angie. Hopefully, the Angies of the future will receive the type of support from the state that they deserve. Even though you are no longer with us, I pray you know we love and miss you "T-O-O."

THANK YOU

We truly hope you enjoyed this title from Kingston Imperial. Our company prides itself on breaking new authors, as well as working with established ones to create incredible reading content to amplify your literary experience. In an effort to keep our movement going, we urge all readers to leave a review (hopefully positive) and let us know what you think. This will not only spread the word to more readers, but it will allow us the opportunity to continue providing you with more titles to read. Thank you for being a part of our journey and for writing a review.

KINGSTON IMPERIAL

Marvis Johnson — Publisher
Kathy Iandoli — Editorial Director
Joshua Wirth — Designer
Kristin Clifford — Publicist, Finn Partners
Emilie Moran — Publicist, Finn Partners

Contact:
Kingston Imperial
144 North 7th Street #255
Brooklyn, NY 11249
Email: Info@kingstonimperial.com
www.kingstonimperial.com